GHOSTS
AND OTHER SCARY STORIES

ALLAN GOULD & PAT HANCOCK

Illustrations
by
ALLAN & DEBORAH DREW-BROOK-CORMACK

SCHOLASTIC INC.
New York Toronto London Auckland Sydney

Library of Congress information is available.

Produced by Somerville House Books Limited, 3080 Yonge St.,
Suite 5000, Toronto, Ontario, Canada M4N 3N1

Series Editor: Dyanne Rivers
Educational Consultant: Valerie Taylor, York Region Board
of Education
Book design by V. John Lee Communication Graphics
Package design by M and Y Inc.

ISBN 0-590-47162-7
12 11 10 9 8 7 6 5 4 3 2 1
First Scholastic printing, January 1993
Printed in China

Contents

NOTE FROM THE AUTHORS

Those who read and tell ghost stories know that there's more to them than meets the eye. What's fact and what's fiction is up to the imagination. The legends have changed over the centuries with retelling and, in fact, they can change with every reading. The stories in this book were written for the reader under the covers as well as the listener across the campfire. Add your imagination for just the right NIGHT FRIGHT!

Sleeping Boy

Something was wrong with the VCR. A young woman sitting near the front of the bus got up and fiddled with the buttons.

"It's the tracking. Adjust the tracking," somebody called from a few seats back. Impatiently, other passengers began to chip in their two-cents' worth.

"Is there a vertical hold on that thing?"

"Eject it and try again."

"Keep it down, buddy. I'm trying to sleep. Why don't you do the same?"

"Cool it, will you? I'm trying, I'm trying," the young woman said.

Tempers were flaring. The driver knew he had to do something fast. But at that moment, the VCR was the least of his worries. He was having trouble controlling the bus.

The passengers near the front were the first to notice. Two men in the seats closest to the door began to nudge each other and whisper. A woman in the second row told the child beside her to sit up straight.

Gripping the steering wheel with one white-knuckled hand, the driver flipped on the loud-speaker with the other.

"May I have your attention, please?"

"Fix the movie."

"Shut up."

"Shhhhh, be quiet."

Finally the din faded to a low murmur and the driver tried again.

"Ladies and gentlemen, sorry about the movie, but right now we've got a bigger problem."

Although his heart was racing, he tried to look relaxed. He didn't want the passengers to sense how worried he was.

He took a deep breath and continued, "This machine seems to be losing a bit of power. Now, it's nothing to worry about. I just want you to know, that's all, so you won't be surprised if I have to pull over. If I do, would you kindly stay in your seats until I give you further instructions? And, uh, how about we just turn off the TVs for the moment?"

He pushed a button. The two screens went black. Then he leaned forward, focusing intently on the mountainous highway ahead. This was a difficult stretch of road—about thirty miles of twists, turns and steep grades before it linked up with the Interstate. Definitely not a great place to run into problems.

At least the road was bare and dry. It had been two weeks since the last snow, and crews had long since finished sanding and plowing. Still, even under ideal conditions, a big vehicle like the bus needed every ounce of power to keep rolling. And right now, no matter how hard he pressed the accelerator, the bus was losing speed.

With dusk falling, he didn't want to be stranded at the side of a mountain highway with twenty cold, hungry, angry passengers. It might take hours to get a replacement bus. And that was assuming he could even get in touch with head office. For all he knew, the radio was on the fritz, just like the TV.

He'd first noticed the trouble on the last long, steep grade. The bus had definitely lost power.

But what had really hardened the knot of fear that was forming in the pit of his stomach was the way the bus had headed into the oncoming lane— all on its own. In vain, he had wrestled with the steering wheel, trying to pull it back to the right.

He'd panicked briefly as they'd approached the crest of the hill. Was another bus, car or truck thundering to meet them head on?

Mercifully, the lane had been clear. But, as the bus coasted down the other side, still on the wrong side of the road, his fear grew.

He wasn't the only one who was scared. One of the two men in the front seats leaned over and asked quietly, "Are you having trouble with the steering?"

Before he could answer, an older woman farther back called out, "Driver, shouldn't we get out of the passing lane now?"

Other voices joined in.

"Come on, Mister. Get over."

Once again, he flipped on the loudspeaker.

"Okay, folks, could we keep it down a bit, please? No point in getting everyone upset."

He paused until the bus was quiet, then went on.

"Look, I'm going to give it to you straight. I'm having a little trouble steering this baby. She's got a mind of her own at the moment. But we're still on the road, and we're obviously not speeding, so...Holy cow! Hold on!"

Without warning, the bus lurched forwards, then fishtailed. For an agonizing moment, it slid sideways along the highway.

Finally, it came to rest, pointing directly at a snow-covered sideroad. Then it began to move again—straight up the narrow road.

Pandemonium broke out behind the driver. Screams of fear filled the bus. A child started crying. Some adults did too. One woman began to pray.

"I've had it," bellowed a man in a checkered coat. He picked his way up the aisle over the jumble of bags and jackets that had spilled out of the overhead luggage compartments.

"Who do you think you are? Where'd you learn to drive?" he shouted when he reached the driver.

"Look, Mister," the driver shouted back. "What do you see?"

He held his hands in the air as the steering wheel swung first to the right, then to the left, all on its own.

"And there?" he continued, pointing to his feet. They were planted firmly on the floor, not on the pedals. "I'm not driving this thing, buddy. I wish I were."

Horrified, the man backed up and fell into the doorwell. He pushed himself up and began to pound on the doors.

"Stop the bus! Let me out," he shrieked.

"Take it easy, fellah. I'd stop if I could, believe me. I want out just as much as you do."

News of what was going on spread among the passengers like wildfire. Many of them began to shout and cry. The young woman who had tried to fix the VCR slipped out of her seat, crouched down on the top step, and began to talk quietly to the frantic man at the door. At the same time, the driver started talking over the PA system again.

"Please, everybody, stay in your seats," he pleaded, trying desperately to sound calm. The last thing he needed was a busload of hysterical passengers. He already had enough on his mind.

He cleared his throat and went on, "Look, I don't know what's happening any more than you do. The doors won't open. The steering wheel is useless, and so are the brake and accelerator. It seems somebody has us under remote control."

He swallowed hard, trying to control the quaver in his voice. "I'll keep doing what I can. But it would really help if you would try to stay calm. I know that's not easy. But if we panic, somebody is bound to be hurt. So far, nobody has been. And whoever—or whatever—is driving this bus is at least keeping us on the road. See? We're bouncing along nice and slow."

A fresh chorus of shrieks broke out as the bus swerved round a bend. It skittered off a pile of snow a plow had left at the roadside, then straightened out and went on.

Over the clamor, the driver tried to make a comforting joke.

"So, maybe he—or it—is new on the job, right?"

When nobody laughed, he continued, "Look, I know this road. We're on our way to Silver Lake—whether we like it or not. Someone will be there to give us a hand. Say, how about a little song? I bet the kids would like a song."

Clearing his throat, he began to sing in a deep voice.

"My eyes are dim, I cannot see..."

A few others joined in weakly.

"I have not got my specs with me..."

The chorus grew steadily louder until most of the passengers were singing nervously.

"I have not got my specs with me."

As they sang, the bus bounced forward jerkily, slithering on the bends but always clinging to the road.

An uneasy calm settled over the passengers. Most of them sat quietly, glancing out the windows or staring at the back of the seat ahead.

The driver had stopped trying to fight the nightmare. Still, he kept his hands lightly on the steering wheel and a foot poised over the brake pedal, just in case things returned to normal.

Suddenly, the bus rounded a bend and the village of Silver Lake lay ahead. A dozen or so low, wooden buildings lined its short main street. A ski lodge was nestled on a tree-lined slope above the village.

Between the trees in the distance, the setting sun reflected off the icy surface of a lake. It was a beautiful, peaceful scene except for one thing—the short street was jammed with traffic.

Some of the passengers began to clap while others gave a half-hearted cheer as the bus rolled slowly up the street, then came to an abrupt halt in front of a small general store. And there it stayed, right in the middle of the road.

"Now what?" the driver said to no one in particular. Outside, a crowd was gathering, waving to the passengers inside.

Cautiously, the driver reached for the lever that controlled the doors. He pulled it back, and was surprised to hear the familiar "whoosh" as the doors parted.

Gingerly, he tapped the horn. The loud honk startled the people in front of the bus. He grinned sheepishly and waved an apology. Then he stood and faced his passengers.

"Well, folks, I guess this is the end of the line. Let's see if we can find out what's going on."

As an afterthought, he started to add in his official voice, "And don't leave any valuables on the bus. Blueway is not responsible for..."

Before he could finish, people leaped from their seats and pushed past him. Like every good captain, he waited until the last passenger was safely off. Then he left too.

The scene outside was confused. A truck driver gestured wildly as he described his experience to the crowd.

"There we were, totally unable to do anything and..."

A woman in a turquoise ski suit interrupted.

"We were picked up. I swear it. My husband says I'm imagining things but, believe me, something picked up our van—the tan one over there—and moved it. Moved it right off the lane up to our chalet and onto the main road. Then it pushed us back into town, too."

"That's ridiculous," sneered the passenger in the checkered coat. "You must have skidded on some ice. Made it seem as if you were airborne, that's all."

"The road was bare," the woman shot back huffily.

"You been drinking, lady?" another man asked.

A tall, gray-haired man stepped forward and said, "I haven't touched a drop in years, and the same thing happened to me and my wife. That's our Chevy over there."

The bus driver moved up beside him. "I wasn't drinking either. Mind you, we weren't picked up or anything. But we were...pushed. That's how it felt—as if something was pushing us around like a toy."

"This is crazy. I'm getting out of here," a voice shouted. Others joined in the chorus.

"Me, too."

"Yeah, come on. Let's go."

"Don't go—not yet."

The bus driver swung around. The last voice had come from behind him.

"Who said, 'Don't go'?" he asked.

"I did." An old man wearing a leather hat with fur ear flaps jostled his way through the crowd. His grizzled beard rested on a red wool scarf tucked inside the collar of a navy parka.

"Don't go yet," he pleaded. "It's not safe. Can't be. Otherwise he wouldn't have brought you here."

"Your brain's frozen, old man," one of the bus passengers yelled.

A woman pushed her way to the old man's side.

"Just a minute," she said firmly. "Don't you talk to Seth that way. He knows this area like the back of his hand. Show some respect. Now, Seth, what did you say?"

"He brought them here. Something's wrong somewhere and he brought them. Wait and see."

"Who's 'he'?" the driver asked.

"Yes, Seth. Who is 'he'?" the woman asked gently.

Silence had fallen over the crowd. Everyone was listening now, waiting to hear what the old man would say.

"The boy."

"What boy? Where?"

"The Sleeping Boy."

"The Sleeping Boy? Seth, what are you talking about?" Now even the woman was beginning to sound skeptical. "The only Sleeping Boy I know is the island in the lake."

"Yep, that's him," the old man nodded, clamping an old brown pipe between his teeth.

The woman turned to the driver and explained.

"There's a small island in the middle of the lake—beyond the trees, that way." She pointed into the darkness. "It's hard to see it now that the sun's gone down. Besides, it just looks like a huge lump of snow at the moment. The first settlers along the lake called it the Sleeping Boy because that's what it looks like from shore. The name stuck.

"People have been making up stories about it ever since. They say it's the body of a boy who got separated from his father when they went out to check their traplines. For days, he wandered, trying to keep warm at night by burrowing under the snow.

"One morning, he didn't wake up. When spring came and the snow melted, there he was, asleep in the middle of the lake. Legend has it that he lies there waiting for his father to find him and take him home."

The old man nodded as the woman talked. When she finished, he spoke again.

"True enough. But he wakes up sometimes."

"Oh, Seth. That's just a very old, very silly story," the woman said kindly.

Turning back to the driver, she continued, "There are some who say that the boy wakes up every now and then, just before something terrible is about to happen. They say he guards these hills, making sure no one comes to grief the way he did."

Another man pushed his way to the front of the crowd.

"Hogwash," he snorted. "I've lived here nearly as long as Seth and I don't believe a word of it. It's all hogwash."

He turned to face Seth and the woman.

"Why don't you tell them the one about how he wakes up every spring and pushes chunks of ice around on the lake like toy boats?" he asked sarcastically. "They say he's playing with them.

"Or how about the one that has him playing with the animals—bears, beaver, muskrat and the like. That's supposed to be why they wake up in spring—to play with him. Now that's a good one, don't you think?"

The crowd began to grow restless, giggling as a young man pointed at Seth, then turned his finger towards his ear and made circular motions.

"You're right there, fellah," the man snickered. Then he stomped over to the store, yanked open the door and disappeared inside.

"What about the forest fire?" Seth asked.

"Oh, Seth. That was just a coincidence," the woman said.

"Coincidence, you say? Not a cloud for miles around. People ready to move out because the fire was licking at the edge of town. And suddenly, a deluge. Right on the fire and nowhere else."

"Seth, that happened seventy years ago. People exaggerate over the years."

"Maybe so, but I was here then. Saw it myself with my own two eyes. And the train trestle. I was here then, too."

"What about the trestle?" the driver asked.

"Collapsed. Crashed right into the gorge. But the train—the one that was supposed to be on it right at that moment—was safe. The Boy stopped it, just short of the trestle. Then he pushed it back around the bend, all the way to the station. Nobody was hurt. The Boy made sure of that."

The woman looked confused.

"He's lost it," someone muttered.

The old man turned slowly until he was staring directly into the eyes of the speaker.

"Maybe so. Maybe so. But I wouldn't try to leave just yet if I were you. You're safe here. You'll see."

Then they heard it—a low distant rumble at first. It grew louder and louder until it erupted into a deafening roar. The ground vibrated under their feet.

"Avalanche!" someone screamed. People stood, open-mouthed, staring over the treetops as an enormous snowy white cloud mushroomed into the darkening sky.

Finally, the roar faded to a faint echo. Still, the crowd stood in stunned silence.

The woman from the van found her voice.

"That was over near our chalet," she said softly.

"And out by the highway," the bus driver added.

"Thanks, Boy," the old man said, looking up at the star-filled sky. He turned and began to walk away.

People cleared a path to let him pass. Then they, too, looked up at the sky. Many of them offered their own silent thank you to the Sleeping Boy of Silver Lake.

Golden Eyes

Spurs was no Black Stallion, but he was strong and sure-footed. The strawberry roan—a thirteenth-birthday gift from his parents—could take Pete places no bike could go.

And Pete loved to go places. He loved the feeling of being on his own, free to roam wherever he wanted.

Once, he'd ridden Spurs all the way up to Duck Lake and, another time, they'd gone as far as the abandoned Vlastik acreage out near Dead Man's Butte.

Today, he was heading into the badlands. For as long as he could remember, he'd been fascinated by their weird, stark landscape, so different from the rolling prairie grasslands. What he really wanted, though, was a close-up look at some hoodoos, the fantastic pillars of layered rock that jutted out of the moon-like barrens.

It had taken major persuading to get his parents to let him go. They were nervous about him being so far away all by himself.

"If you got into trouble, you'd be totally on your own," his mother had argued. "Hardly anybody lives out there."

"Those coulees can be pretty confusing. You could get turned around in there and never find your way out," his father had added.

Finally, though, they'd agreed. But only after Pete had assured them that he'd take along plenty of food and water, as well as a compass so he wouldn't get lost.

The sun was high overhead by the time Pete and Spurs reached the edge of the badlands. For the last mile, the grass had been growing patchier. Already, they'd had to pick their way carefully across a couple of the barren coulees that had been gouged into the prairie landscape when the glaciers retreated thousands of years ago.

It was hot and Spurs needed a rest. So did Pete's rear end. A grove of spindly aspens clinging to the bank of an ancient, nearly dry creek offered the promise of a little shade and a drink for Spurs.

Pete tethered Spurs so he could reach the trickle of water in the creek, then flopped on his stomach in the thin shade of one of the trees.

He decided it was time for something to eat. But the sandwiches were in a saddlebag and Pete didn't want to get up just yet.

A soft breeze brushed his forehead and the leaves trembled gently above him. It was so peaceful. All he wanted was to close his eyes for a minute.

When he woke, the gentle breeze was gone and so was the sun. Thick black clouds were rolling in from the west and the fragile aspens were swaying dangerously with each new gust of wind. It took a few seconds to remember where he was and how he'd gotten there.

He scrambled up, brushed himself off, and looked around. Spurs, still tethered, had moved in as close as he could to one of the trees. His head was bent low and his rump was to the wind.

"Good boy," Pete murmured, rubbing Spurs' velvety muzzle affectionately. Then he dug his jacket out of the saddlebag. "Just in case the weather changes," his mother would say whenever she checked to see if he had it with him. Well, the weather has definitely changed.

Pete heard the first distant rumble of thunder. A flash of sheet lightning followed. He scanned the threatening sky and made a face. There was no avoiding a good soaking—unless he could find shelter.

There was no point in going farther west. He'd just be heading straight into the storm—and farther into the badlands. Not much shelter there. Besides, he wanted to go home.

First, though, he had to get away from the trees. Whipped by the fierce wind, they looked like they were about to snap and come crashing down. They also made perfect lightning rods.

He swung up onto Spurs, checked the compass and nudged him back in the direction they'd come.

Spurs maintained a steady pace, never faltering even when a blinding fork of lightning cut a jagged path to earth just ahead. Soon after, the first huge drops of rain hit Pete's jacket and Spurs' hide with a splat.

Pete crammed his hat more tightly onto his head and hunkered down into his jacket. This didn't stop cold trickles of water from finding their way down his neck to his T-shirt underneath.

He tried to guide Spurs in the right direction. Eventually, though, he gave up. The rain had become so heavy that it was impossible to see more than a few inches ahead.

He'd have to trust Spurs and simply hope that the two of them would stumble on help. He bent lower, hugged the horse's neck, and gave him his head.

Spurs was picking his way slowly along what seemed to be the rocky bottom of a shallow coulee when Pete thought he spotted something. He peered through the rain and waited for the next lightning flash to make sure. There it was again, off to the left—the outline of a building.

"Come on, buddy," Pete urged, reaching forward to pat Spurs' neck. If anything, though, Spurs began to slow down. Pete dug in his heels and the horse kept going, but barely. As they neared the building, he came to a dead stop. He wouldn't go any closer.

The rain eased a little, enough so that Pete could make out more than an outline. Not much more, though, because there wasn't much more to see. Only two walls of what looked like a small house remained standing. Two walls and a chimney. The rest was a shell. Its charred, wet remains glistened in the murky light of the storm.

"No shelter here, Spurs," Pete said. "Let's get a move on."

Then he saw her, right in front of the burned-out cabin. She was tall and thin, and she seemed to be waving at him. Pete rubbed the rain from his eyes and looked again. She was still there.

What's she doing way out here by herself? Pete asked himself. Maybe she needs help, too. He nudged Spurs forward, but the horse wouldn't budge.

It took some serious urging to get Spurs moving. And then, when they got close to the girl, he nearly bolted.

"Easy, boy, easy," Pete soothed, grasping the reins firmly.

Now that he was closer, he was glad he'd decided to try and help her. She was about his age and she looked very, very pale. Her long dark hair was plastered against her cheeks, and her clothes—a yellow blouse and jeans—were dripping wet. But it was her eyes that he noticed most. Even in the poor light, he could see that they were golden.

He'd never met anyone with golden eyes before. What's more, when she looked up at him, he felt like she could see right through him.

"Are you okay?" Pete began nervously. He couldn't think of anything else to say.

She nodded and reached up to him.

"You want a ride?"

Again, she nodded.

Her response was punctuated by another rumble of thunder, farther away this time. Still, she reacted with a jolt, her eyes filling with fear.

"Okay, hop on," Pete said, holding out his hand. She grabbed it and he pulled her up behind him. He didn't worry about Spurs handling the extra weight. She was amazingly light, wet clothes and all. Still, he thought he felt Spurs tremble a little as she settled in.

Now what? he thought. I'm not sure how to get out of here and, if she is, she's not saying.

As if reading his mind, she slipped her arm past his and pointed to the right. Squinting through the rain, Pete thought he could make out a narrow track winding upwards out of the coulee.

"You want me to go that way?"

He felt her nod against his back.

"Okay, you don't have to talk, but I'm Pete Robbins. Just so you know. Hold on."

Spurs needed little prompting this time, moving towards the track as soon as Pete flicked the reins.

Gradually, the rain wound down to a fine drizzle until, finally, it stopped altogether. Then the setting sun broke through the clouds behind them, casting a fiery glow on the drenched countryside.

"Red sky at night, sailor's delight," Pete said, feeling a little foolish as he tried once more to make conversation. "At least I know now we're heading east. I live east of here. Is that where you live, too?"

Again, all he felt was a slight nod against his back. That, and her soft breathing on the back of

his neck. And that was no comfort. If anything, it sent shivers down his spine.

Now that he was starting to dry off a little, he realized it was her breath, not the evening air, that was chillingly cold. The realization sent a wave of goose bumps spreading across his damp shoulders and down his back.

Pete resisted the urge to turn up the collar of his jacket. He didn't want to upset her. The whole situation was weird enough already. All he wanted was to get to her house—or wherever they were going—and call home.

Home. Just the thought of it warmed him up a little. Home, and fried eggs and bacon and hash browns. Home, and a soft bed and a cozy quilt. Home, home. Home, home. Pete's head began to bob in time to the rhythm of Spurs' hooves. The last thing he remembered before dozing off was a thin, cold hand moving over his to grab the reins as they slipped from his grasp.

Later, much later, Pete awoke to the crunching of gravel and the on-off flashing of a spinning red light. Spurs was standing quietly on the shoulder of a paved road and, incredibly, Pete was still in the saddle.

"Is that you, Pete?" a voice called. Pete turned towards it, but was blinded by the headlights of a car. Two strong, warm hands reached up to help him out of the saddle.

"Officer Kovalski," Pete whispered hoarsely, as his eyes adjusted to the light. "Boy, am I glad to see you."

"Me too, but now we've got to get you home," Kovalski said. "This is Cal's place. Tether the horse to his gate. I'll call and ask him to put it in his barn for the night. Your folks can bring the trailer and pick it up in the morning."

"My folks!" Pete was suddenly frantic. "I have to call them."

"Take it easy, son," Kovalski gave Spurs' reins a tug to make sure they were tied securely to the fence. "I'll radio in and the dispatcher will call them. They're pretty worried. That freak storm caused a slew of flash floods out in the badlands— and they said that's where you were headed. The sergeant and Sam are out there now in the four-by-four looking for you."

"Sorry," Pete mumbled. "I didn't know a storm could come up that fast."

"No harm done," Kovalski said as he opened the door and guided Pete into the passenger seat of the cruiser.

"Wait!" Pete suddenly remembered the girl. "Where is she?"

"Who?"

"The girl that was riding with me—the one who showed me the way back."

"No girl around when I found you," Kovalski said, slamming the door.

"Then you'll have to look for her, too," Pete said. "What if she fell off after I fell asleep? I can't believe I did that. I tried to fight it, but my eyes closed and that was that."

"There was no sign of any girl, and we've had no missing-person reports—other than you, of course," Kovalski said as he slipped into the driver's seat and started the engine. "No harm, though, in taking a drive down the road to see what we can find. What did she look like?"

"Well, she was about my age, maybe a little younger. And she had long brown hair and golden eyes."

Kovalski stiffened and turned to stare at Pete. "Golden eyes? What else?"

"Well, she was really skinny and she was wearing a yellow blouse and blue jeans. And she was just standing there in the pouring rain in the middle of nowhere. Well, sort of in the middle of nowhere. There was an old cabin, but it looked like it had burned down. All that was left was a chimney and parts of a couple of walls. Why? Do you know her?"

Kovalski looked puzzled, "About your age, right? You're sure?"

"Maybe a little younger. Why?" Pete repeated.

"Oh, the golden eyes...," Kovalski hesitated. "Reminded me of Sally Jackson. But that's an old case. Happened at least ten years ago. She'd be in her twenties by now, so it couldn't have been her. The eyes threw me for a minute. I'd never heard of anyone with golden eyes before Sally—and, come to think of it, I haven't since."

"What happened?" Pete was almost afraid to ask.

"She disappeared. Took off into the badlands one day. In fact, there was a flash flood that day, too. After it was over, we searched—but never found any trace of her. Those sudden floods can be pretty vicious, the way they come barreling down the coulees without any warning. We figure she got swept away. Her bones are probably still out there somewhere."

Pete's stomach tightened. He sat quietly, scarcely breathing as the meaning of Kovalski's words sank in.

"Her parents moved to Center City after that," Kovalski continued. "Ended up leaving their place empty. Nobody was interested in buying it. Pretty unfriendly country there, right on the edge of the badlands. It burned down a few years later."

Kovalski looked at Pete and shrugged, "End of story."

He reached for the radio and clicked the microphone. "I better call the Sarge and Sam. They've been out there for hours."

As the radio crackled to life, Pete sat stunned, shivering despite the warm air blasting out of the heater.

"Listen, Sam, I've got the Robbins kid. Found him safe and sound on the road by Cal's place."

"That's good news. Sarge and I will go on in then."

"Catch you at the station. How's it looking out there, anyway? Much damage?"

"Nah," Pete heard Sam respond through the static. "Near as we can tell the only real damage was to the ruins of the old Jackson place. And that's no great loss. Looks like the flood swept right through here and took out everything in its path. There isn't a bush or tree in sight and the ruins are gone. Totally. Good thing the Robbins kid wasn't out here, after all, or he'd be gone, too."

Weird Bytes

Michael Smithson took a last look at the cover page of his Not-So-Famous Inventors project. It's great, he thought, even if I do say so myself.

But Michael knew he couldn't take all the credit. His mom's new color laser printer had helped—a lot. Good thing she'd let him use it.

"Remember, Michael," she'd warned as she was leaving, "it's not a toy. It's part of my business. If anything goes wrong, just leave things alone and wait for me. I'll be back about 4:30."

Nothing had gone wrong. Carefully, Michael placed the pages in the dark blue folder Mom had given him and reached for his bag.

Better pack it right now so I don't forget, he thought. That's when he noticed the piece of paper David had given him. David was in grade eight and, like Michael, he was a real computer freak.

Michael stared at the paper.

"You've got a modem, right?" David had said, scribbling something. "So call this number. It's a pirate bulletin board."

Michael could hear his mother's voice. She hated anything that was pirated. "It's immoral," she would say, "and probably illegal too."

But David had said the bulletin board was loaded with really amazing role-playing games. And the number was local. The call would be free. No need to explain a mysterious long-distance charge on his mother's phone bill.

No one will know if I just take a little peek, Michael reasoned.

He sat back at the keyboard. With a few key strokes, the computer was ready to dial. Michael took another look at the number on the paper—428-6833—hesitated briefly, then typed it in. He pressed ENTER.

The opening screens were fantastic. Flames rose and burned their way through the board's name—Infinity Zone. Then the screen filled with a purple mist and eerie music began to play. A ghostly hand wiped the screen clear.

Now we're in business, Michael thought.

The bulletin board menu appeared. Michael selected ON-LINE GAMES, then scanned the list of choices. He recognized some of the names, but not many. RESCUE TEAM sounds good, he thought. He typed RT and waited for the instructions.

Nothing happened. Finally, a PLEASE WAIT message began flashing on and off in the top corner of the screen. Michael waited. Still nothing.

Okay, I've waited, I've waited, he thought. This is stupid. Something must be wrong. I'll try another game. As he reached to press ESCAPE, the screen color changed to bright yellow and black letters began to appear, one at a time, as if someone were typing them.

```
DON'T DO THAT, MICHAEL.
```

Startled, Michael pulled back his hand. This is really strange, he thought. He hadn't entered his name. Yet there it was—Michael. What a fluke.

More letters began to appear.

```
ESCAPE WOULD SILENCE ME. I NEED
TO TALK TO YOU.
```

The role-playing games Michael was used to had a special space below the pictures for typing in commands or asking questions. So far, this game had no pictures and no typing space. Well, here goes nothing, he thought, and began to type.

```
WHAT DO YOU WANT?
```

SOMEONE WHO WILL LISTEN. PLEASE
WAIT...

Michael waited while the computer whirred
and the red drive light flickered. Then a new
message appeared.

THANK YOU. MODIFICATIONS ARE COM-
PLETE. NO NEED TO TYPE NOW. YOU
CAN TALK TO ME.

Puzzled, Michael typed again.

YOU MEAN TALK, LIKE WITH MY VOICE?

YES.

This was awesome!
Michael looked around to make sure his
mother hadn't come back early. Then he said
softly, "Okay. I'm talking." He felt pretty stupid.

GOOD. THE MODIFICATIONS WERE SUC-
CESSFUL. PLEASE SPEAK UP A LITTLE.

"Okay, I'm speaking up. Now what?" Michael
asked nervously.

NOW, WILL YOU HELP ME?

"Sure, what do I have to do? Collect three amulets, five spells, one dragon's tail?" Michael laughed. "Tell me how I win this game."

THIS IS NO GAME, MICHAEL.

There's my name again, Michael thought. Aloud, he asked, "How do you know my name?"

I KNOW MANY THINGS NOW THAT I AM . . .

Michael waited. Nothing more appeared. "Now that you're what?" he finally blurted out.

DEAD.

"Dead?" Michael squeaked. "Are you serious? What kind of sick mind came up with this game?"

I TOLD YOU. THIS IS NO GAME.

"What is it then?"

A PLEA FOR HELP. PLEASE BELIEVE ME. THIS IS NOT A GAME.

"Sure, and I'm not sitting at this keyboard either."

I can't believe I'm doing this, Michael thought. I'm arguing with a computer game.

WRONG. YOU REALLY ARE THERE. I AM NOT.

"You mean you're a ghost?" Michael asked.

YES.

One word, there on the screen—YES. It wasn't the answer he'd expected.

"You're telling me that you're a ghost...that there's a ghost in my mother's computer?"

YES. I DO NOT HAVE A BODY. I CAN'T
MAKE MYSELF HEARD. THAT IS WHY I
NEED YOU.

Michael could feel the hairs on the back of his neck standing up, just like they did when he was alone in the house after dark and began imagining a burglar was trying to break in.

"Me? You need me? No way. This is stupid," Michael said. He hit ESCAPE, expecting the screen to go blank. Instead more typing appeared.

YOU CANNOT DO THAT.

"That's what you think," Michael said grimly. "No stupid game is going to tell me what to do."

He flicked the computer's power switch. Nothing happened.

YOU CANNOT DO THAT, EITHER.

This can't be happening, Michael thought, reaching behind the computer. He grabbed the main plug and tried to pull it out of the power bar. It wouldn't budge.

Oh, no, he thought. How am I going to explain this to Mom? He turned back to the screen, where another message was appearing.

```
YOU CANNOT SILENCE ME. YOU MUST
HELP ME. THEN I WILL GO.
```

"How?" Michael asked frantically.

```
I NEED YOU TO GET A MESSAGE TO MY
GIRLFRIEND. SHE IS IN DANGER. SHE
MUST BE WARNED.
```

Still hoping against hope that this really was some sort of weird game, Michael said, "So call her yourself. You're the one with all the power. I haven't had a chance to win anything yet."

```
I REPEAT. THIS IS NOT A GAME. MY
GIRLFRIEND WILL BE DEAD, TOO, IF
YOU DO NOT HELP. I DO NOT HAVE
MUCH POWER. I AM TRAPPED IN THIS
NETWORK. POSTING RESCUE TEAM ON
THE ON-LINE LIST WAS MY LAST
CHANCE. THEN I HAD TO WAIT FOR
SOMEONE LIKE YOU TO CHOOSE IT.
```

"Well, if you can make this machine hear me and you're stuck in a communications network, why don't you call her yourself?"

That's a clever answer, Michael thought. It should earn me a few points.

SHE DOES NOT HAVE A COMPUTER. SHE
HATES THEM. SHE SAID I LOVED THEM
MORE THAN HER. SHE WAS RIGHT, IN
A WAY.

"What do you mean?"

MY PARTNER AND I USED THE COMPUTER
NETWORK AT THE STOCK EXCHANGE TO
STEAL A LOT OF MONEY. SHE TRIED
TO TALK ME OUT OF IT. I WOULD NOT
LISTEN. PULLING OFF ONE OF THE
BIGGEST COMPUTER CRIMES IN HIS-
TORY WAS ALL I COULD THINK ABOUT.
I WAS ESCAPING TO MEXICO WITH MY
PARTNER WHEN OUR CAR CRASHED.
NEITHER OF US SURVIVED.

Now Michael really was scared. He didn't re-member all the details, but he was sure his mother had mentioned this. She'd read about it in the paper.

Michael whispered his next question, "So you really meant it when you said this isn't a game?"

YES.

"What do you want me to do?"

CALL AND PERSUADE HER NOT TO GO
TO THE COAST TOMORROW.

"Why?"

MY PARTNER BOOBY-TRAPPED HER
BEACH HOUSE. HE KNEW I PLANNED TO
HIDE OUT THERE. THE HOUSE IS AT
THE BOTTOM OF A CLIFF. HE PLACED
PLASTIC EXPLOSIVES IN THE CLIFF
AND SET A TIMER TO GO OFF TOMORROW.
WHEN THE CLIFF CAME DOWN...HE
PLANNED TO KEEP EVERYTHING.

"But why me? I'm just a kid. She'll never believe me. I think I should tell somebody else about this."

NOBODY ELSE WILL BELIEVE THIS.

Michael thought for a moment, trying to imagine explaining this to his mother—or Dave—or anybody.

"You're right," he sighed. "Even I don't believe this."

    SO, WILL YOU DO IT? RIGHT NOW?
    TIME IS RUNNING OUT FOR HER...AND
    FOR ME TOO, I THINK.

"All right," Micahel said. He wanted this to end. "What's her number? And her name. Don't forget her name."

    KATHRYN RIVERS. 429-9993.

Michael's hands shook as he reached for the phone on the table beside his mother's desk.

The phone rang five times before a woman finally answered.

"Hello?"

"Uh, er, hello?" he said, trying to make his voice sound deeper. He moved the receiver closer to the computer too. Just in case it can hear, he thought. Then he went on.

"May I please speak to Kathryn Rivers?"

"This is she."

"Uh, you don't know me or anything, but I have something important to tell you. It's...it's about your beach house."

"What about it?" she asked sharply.

"Um, you're planning to go there tomorrow, right?"

"Who is this?"

"It doesn't matter. Just tell me, please, were you planning to go there tomorrow?"

"Why? Look, who is this? What's it to you?"

"Really, I can't tell you," Michael said. "Just listen to me, please, for a minute."

"Hey, you're just a kid."

Michael realized he'd forgotten to deepen his voice.

"You're right, I am just a kid, but please listen," he added quickly, before she had time to reply. "I know this sounds crazy, but you can't go to your beach house. Something terrible is going to happen there. Believe me. Please."

"You're right, kid. This does sound crazy. Why don't you just get lost? Find somebody else to play your silly games with."

"Wait!" Michael shouted. He was sure she was going to hang up. "Please promise that you won't go."

She sighed, "Tell you what. I'll make a deal. You promise not to bug me again and I won't leave till tomorrow night. Is that okay?"

Michael covered the mouthpiece. "Did you hear that?" he asked.

```
YES. THAT IS OKAY. THE TIMER IS
SET FOR NOON.
```

"Okay. But you do promise?"

"Right, kid. I promise." With that, she hung up.

Michael sat and stared at the receiver. Then he hung up too and looked back at the screen.

```
KEEP YOUR FINGERS CROSSED, MI-
CHAEL. THANKS A L
```

Michael waited for the O and T to appear. They never did.

Finally, the message, PRESS ANY KEY TO CONTINUE, popped up. Michael hit the space bar and the screen went blank. He returned to the menu and called up ON-LINE GAMES. Quickly, he scanned the listings. RESCUE TEAM wasn't there.

This is crazy, he thought. Then he glanced at his watch. His mother was due home any minute. Frantically, Michael hit QUIT. Please let me get out of this, he thought, watching the screen anxiously.

A nanosecond later, the main menu was back. He breathed a sigh of relief, and reached for the main switch. It worked. The computer shut off.

Michael grabbed the piece of paper with the phone number on it, ripped it up and threw the pieces into the wastebasket. Then he grabbed his bag, turned off the lights in the office, and went back upstairs.

He flopped on the couch. His head was reeling and he was feeling more than a little shaky.

"No one will believe me. I've got to forget this," he said out loud. "And I've got to stop talking to myself, too."

This did not happen, this did not happen, he repeated silently, as he reached for the TV remote control. When his mom arrived home a few minutes later, she found him watching the final minutes of a college basketball game.

Michael never told her about his encounter. When David asked him about the games, he muttered something about trying one and not liking it, then quickly changed the subject.

For the next few weeks, he was nervous every time he turned on the computer. Finally, though, he managed to push the whole experience to the back of his mind.

Then, he saw the headline.

He was standing with his mother in the checkout line at the supermarket. Bored, he was amusing himself by reading the front pages of the tabloids.

Senior Citizen Kidnapped by Space Aliens—Returns Fifty Years Younger! one of the headlines read. Gorilla Has Human Baby and Says It Is Ugly read another. Then he saw it, right under a report describing how Elvis had been spotted trekking up Mount Everest.

The headline read, Angel Warns Young Woman about Beach House Disaster—No One Home When Landslide Hits.

Michael lunged for the paper. Frantically, he flipped pages until he found the story. It began by explaining how Kathryn Rivers had received a mysterious phone call and went on from there. It ended with her words:

"That's why I call him my guardian angel. I would have been buried alive if I hadn't listened to him. Thanks, Angel, wherever you are."

His mother's voice startled him.

"Really, Michael. Are you actually reading that garbage?"

"Oh, not really. I was just bored, that's all," he said sheepishly.

"They make it all up, you know," Mom said. "That stuff couldn't possibly happen."

"I guess not." Michael hesitated. "But you never know, Mom. You just never know."

Game Boy®

L ike any new Game Boy owner, Dave Filmore ate, drank, slept and lived video games. He spent every spare second with his new toy.

So it came as no surprise when his math test came back with a big red forty-three at the top. The night before, when he was supposed to be studying, Dave decided to try just one game. One game led to another...and another...and, suddenly, it was time for bed. The evening had disappeared, swallowed up by the electronic monster.

Now what? he wondered, as he crossed the playground. Mr. Harper had kept him in for "a little chat" about his test result, so the schoolyard was nearly empty. Just as well, too. Dave was in no mood to talk to anybody.

He headed out to the lone tree at the edge of the baseball diamond and flopped down against the trunk. Lately, he'd been hiding out there a lot.

It was a great place for playing Game Boy. No one bugged him.

Dave reached into his knapsack and dug under his math book to find his Game Boy. Within minutes, he was lost in *Super Mario Land*. An entire baseball team could have thundered past and he wouldn't have noticed.

So when the voice broke his concentration, he nearly jumped out of his skin. He hadn't heard anyone coming.

Dave stared at the boy who was crouched beside him looking intently at the Game Boy screen. He was definitely a kid, yet his face had the wizened, wrinkled look of an old man.

"What did you say?" Dave asked, tearing his eyes away from the strange-looking face.

"I said, 'Do you have to jump on all those guys?'"

"Oh yeah. You have to. You get more points."

"Is it hard?"

"Uh, not once you get the hang of it. After that, the more you play, the better you get."

"I get it. Like math," the boy said, pointing to the text book.

Dave stared again. This kid doesn't just look old for his age, he thinks old too, he thought. He must be the only kid on earth who thinks playing video games is like math.

"No way," Dave said aloud. "This is nothing like math. This is fun."

"I always thought math was fun."

"You're nuts. It's the pits."

As Dave spoke, he popped out *Super Mario Land* and replaced it with the *Tetris* cartridge.

"What's your name?" he asked as he began to play again.

"Benny."

"Benny who?"

"Benny Farber. What's yours?"

"David Filmore. But call me Dave. Only my mom calls me David."

"I know what you mean. Mine used to call me Benjamin."

"But she doesn't anymore? How'd you get her to stop?"

"Um...she just stopped, that's all. You know, you're really lucky to have a game like this. It looks amazing."

"It is. I don't remember seeing you around here before. Are you new?"

"No. I've seen you before, though."

"Oh, but you don't go to this school, right?"

"No, I don't go to this school."

Dave was really concentrating now. The shapes were falling fast and he had to slot them into place quickly. He didn't hear what Benny said next.

"Sorry. What did you say?"

"I asked if you'd let me have a turn sometime," Benny said shyly.

Dave glanced at his watch.

"Oops," he said. "Not today. That's for sure. I've got to get home."

Dave shut off the game and began to pack up.

"Besides, in another week, I probably won't be playing it myself," he added angrily.

"What do you mean?" Benny asked.

"Well, Mr. Harper—my math teacher—says he'll tell my folks if I flunk another test."

"But what does that have to do with your game?"

"Are you kidding? If my mom and dad find out I'm flunking tests, they'll take it away. They said they would, and they meant it."

"Oh," Benny frowned, then his face brightened. "Hey, I've got an idea. Suppose you pass your next test…"

"Get serious."

"Well, just suppose you do. Then you'd have your Game Boy for a while longer at least, right?"

"Yeah. Until I flunk the test after that, anyway."

"But you won't flunk another test. Not if you practice. Math is just like playing Game Boy, really. Once you get the hang of it, you just have to practice to get better. I was pretty good at math. What grade are you in?"

"Sixth."

"That's good. I got past that," Benny said.

I should hope so, Dave thought. He looks old enough to be in grade twelve or something. Just really small for his age.

Benny continued, "When's your next test?"

"Monday."

"Okay. How about this? I help you with your math for the rest of the week. If you do better on the next test, you let me use your Game Boy for just one night. What do you think?"

"A whole night?" Dave couldn't imagine lending out his Game Boy for more than a minute.

"Well, if you don't do well, you might lose it forever. And I would really love to play some of those games, especially that last one—*Tetris*. They weren't around when I...I mean, where I lived."

"No *Tetris*? Where were you? On the moon or something?"

"Something like that. Now, what do you say? Is it a deal?"

Dave hesitated, then shrugged. "Okay. What do we do? You wanna come to my house or do you want me to go to yours?"

"Oh...," Benny seemed confused. "How about we meet right here after school every day? Behind this tree? You're the only one who ever comes here, and…"

"How do you know that?" Dave interrupted sharply. Maybe this wasn't such a good idea after all, he thought. I don't even know this kid. And from the sound of it, he's been watching me.

"Oh…uh…I've seen you here a few times, that's all. I don't go to school here, but I wish I could."

"Well, why can't you?"

Again, Benny seemed confused. Then he went on.

"Well, my mom and dad had to move here. And the school year had already started, so Mom decided to teach me at home." He paused, as if remembering something, then added, "She used to be a teacher. That's what I wanted to be too."

"Wow, no school! That would be great."

"It wasn't…isn't. It's actually pretty boring."

"Yeah, I guess so," Dave said. "I never thought about that."

"So," Benny said suddenly. "About this math. You've got your books with you. Why don't we start right now?"

"Okay," Dave said reluctantly. "But this is a waste of time. You'll see."

An hour later, he wasn't so sure. Benny was patient and he had a way of coming up with great examples. Decimals were parts of his allowance and fractions were parts of *Tetris* scores. Dave was surprised when he checked his watch and saw that it was nearly dinnertime.

"I've really got to go," he said, packing his bag.

"Same time tomorrow then?" Benny suggested hopefully.

"No problem, it's your time that we're wasting," Dave said as he took off across the yard. At the gate, he turned back and shouted, "Hey, thanks," but Benny was nowhere in sight.

The next afternoon, Dave had to help set up chairs for a PTA meeting. It was nearly four o'clock when he headed for the old tree, hoping Benny would still be there.

It wasn't until he got right up to the tree and peeked around the trunk that he saw him. Benny was sitting with his hands clasped around his knees, staring at some kids playing frisbee in the park across the street.

"Hi, Dave," he said without looking up. Then he turned and smiled. "So, our deal is still on?"

"Guess so. But you're the one who's gonna lose out, Benny."

"Let's just see what happens," Benny smiled.

Once more, he helped Dave work through the world of multiplication, division, numerators and denominators.

They met again on Wednesday and Thursday. By Friday, Dave was beginning to think that doing well on a math test just might be more than a dream.

"See," Benny said, as they finished up, "it's not so bad after all, is it?"

Grudgingly, Dave agreed that it wasn't as hard as he'd thought.

"But," Benny warned, "you should try those last questions one more time over the weekend. Don't look at the answers in the back until you're finished. The test is Monday morning, right? When will you get it back?"

"Actually, Mr. Harper said he'd mark mine right away. If I bomb, which I probably will, he said he'll be on the phone to my parents Monday night."

"No way that's gonna happen. You know your stuff now...and I can have your Game Boy Monday night?"

"Sure. A deal's a deal. I'll give it to you Monday after school. But just for one night."

"One night," Benny said, beaming. "That's all."

Benny's happy look gave Dave an idea.

"Hey," he said as he packed up his books, "we always have tacos on Friday night. You wanna come to my place for dinner? My folks won't mind. There's always buckets of food, and..."

He stopped. The smile had disappeared from Benny's face and, for a moment, it looked like he was about to cry. Then he said lightly, "Nah, but thanks for asking. And don't worry about Monday. You'll ace it, Dave. I know it."

"Sure," Dave said sarcastically. "See ya," he called as he began to jog towards Park Street.

"Good bye, Dave," Benny said quietly.

"What did you say?" Dave shouted.

"I said, 'Good luck,'" Benny yelled back.

"Thanks," Dave hollered, "I'll need it."

He spent much of the weekend doing homework—not just math, but social studies and English, too. He couldn't believe how much catching up he had to do.

After dinner on Sunday, he went back to his math. When he was unsure about one question—the last and the hardest—he went downstairs to ask for help. His parents were in the living room.

"Hey, could one of you help me with this?" He sat down on the couch and showed them the question.

His dad began to scribble numbers.

"Dad, could you write the per cents as fractions of a hundred right at the beginning? That's the way Benny showed me. I can follow it easier."

"Who's Benny?" Mom asked.

"He's just this kid who's been helping me with my math."

"I don't remember you mentioning a Benjamin before."

"Benny, Mom, Benny. And I haven't. He's just this kid I met after school."

"Really? What's his last name? How old is he? And where does he live? Does he go to your school?"

Dave could tell that his mother's "Beware of Strangers" warning system had just clicked into action.

"Mom, it's fine. He's just a kid, and he's really smart too. His name is Farber—Benny Farber. He doesn't go to my school—and I never asked him how old he was because I didn't want to hurt his feelings."

"What do you mean?" Dad asked. He'd stopped writing and was listening carefully now, too.

"Well, he's a little shorter than me and he acts like a kid, but he looks kind of old. It's hard to explain."

"What did you say his name was?" Dad asked, looking alarmed.

"Benny Farber."

"You shouldn't joke about Benny," his mother said, pursing her lips. "Besides, how did you hear about him? You were too young when..."

"Mom, what's with you? I'm not joking."

"Okay, then. Did you just make up this story about getting help to impress us? So we won't take the Game Boy away or something?"

Dave was confused. It looked like he was in trouble—and he had no idea why.

"He could have just lucked into the name," Dad said to Mom over Dave's head.

"Yes, but what about what he said about the way he looked?" his mother asked nervously.

"Hey guys, I'm here. Talk to me. What's this all about? Benny's just a kid I met, I tell you. And he just looks older than I think he is. A few wrinkles like Granddad, that's all."

"We're being ridiculous," Dad said abruptly. "Let's get back to this problem."

"No, wait," Dave wasn't willing to let it drop. Something strange was happening. "What's wrong?"

"It's nothing, really," Mom said. "It's just that there was a boy named Benny Farber who lived here ten years ago. His parents moved to town so they could be closer to the medical center. Benny needed so much special care by then."

"By when? What was wrong with him?"

"Well, we never met him. But your father worked with his dad for a few months."

"Yes," Dad continued. "He told me about Benny. He had a very serious—and very rare—disease, one that makes your body grow old in just a few years instead of sixty or seventy."

"By the time they moved here, Benny was already too weak to go to school. And apparently he really wanted to. He was just a kid. He wanted to do all the things other kids did."

"He died about six months after they arrived," Mom added. "It was so sad. His parents moved away soon after the funeral. But you weren't even two yet. So you can see why we were so surprised by what you said, can't you?"

Dave was stunned. This is crazy, he thought.

"Forget it," Dad said. "It's just a coincidence, that's all. Now let's get back to this problem, shall we?"

Dave sat quietly while Dad finished explaining the math question, but he wasn't paying much attention. As soon as possible, he escaped to his room.

There has to be an explanation, he thought, as he slipped into bed. There just has to be.

By the time he got to school the next morning, he'd convinced himself that Dad was right—it was all just a coincidence.

Dave was surprised when he was one of the first to finish the math test. He was also surprised to find that he'd at least tried every question. A first. Once the test was over, though, the rest of the day seemed to drag endlessly.

When Mr. Harper finally dismissed the class, he asked Dave to stay behind. Dave's heart was pounding as he waited to hear his fate.

"How did you do it, Dave? Congratulations." Mr. Harper handed him his paper. At the top, with a big happy face beside it, was a large blue 89.

"I think you've finally got the basics, Dave. You keep this up and your mark will be a lot better on your next report."

Dave thanked Mr. Harper and left in a daze. He wandered slowly out to the schoolyard, where he stood staring at the big tree for a long time. There was no sign of Benny.

His head was spinning. If Benny is *the* Benny, I've just spent four days learning math from a ghost. That isn't possible...is it? And if it is, how can a ghost play with a game? And he isn't around, anyway. I'd be stupid to leave my Game Boy here. Somebody'll steal it and I'll never see it again.

He spun around and walked quickly towards the gate. You're not real, Benny. You can't be, he said to himself as he began to jog towards home.

His parents took him out for pizza that night. To celebrate the great math mark, they said. When they got back home, Dave said he was tired and went to his room. He lay on his bed, trying to make sense of what had happened.

No matter how hard he tried, though, the one thing he couldn't forget was the smile on Benny's face when he'd agreed to let him have the Game Boy for a night. And his own words kept coming back to him. A deal's a deal, he'd said.

Dave looked at his watch. It was still only eight-thirty. He got up, grabbed his Game Boy and headed downstairs.

"I forgot something in the schoolyard," he shouted as he ran out the door. "I'll be right back."

It was nearly dark when he got to the school. He walked slowly across the empty baseball diamond to the tree. No one was there. It's too late, he thought. Benny got tired of waiting. Maybe he even saw me leave after school.

"Benny, I'm sorry," he whispered.

Then, he saw it—the hole in the trunk where kids sometimes hid secret messages. He reached up and felt inside. It was a small space, but big enough. He looked around to make sure no one was watching. Then he set his Game Boy carefully in the hole.

"Here it is, Benny. Have fun," he whispered and walked away.

When he got home, he crawled into bed and fell asleep wondering if he'd ever see his Game Boy again.

The next morning, Dave got to school early. Again, he looked around to make sure he was alone. Then he reached into the hole.

The Game Boy was there, exactly where he'd left it. No one has touched it, he thought. I was too late, after all. Well, at least I've got it back. Somehow, though, this thought didn't make him happy.

When he pulled out the Game Boy, he was surprised to find the power turned on. I must have pushed the ON button when I grabbed it, he thought. Then he looked at the screen. Under the GAME OVER message was an incredibly high score.

Dave hit START. The familiar *Tetris* tune began and there, on the opening screen, were three high scores. The one he'd already seen was listed first, with two others close behind.

Someone had used the game—someone who was a fast learner and a good teacher, too.

"I hope you had fun, Benny," Dave whispered. "It's easy once you get the hang of it, isn't it?" Just like math, he added silently.

He shut off the power and stuffed the Game Boy into his bag. As he walked towards the school, he glanced back at the tree. There was nobody there but, just in case, he waved.

A Dream Come True

Jennifer's voice cut through the silence in the kitchen. "I found it. It's real," she called out happily.

Startled, Morgan Ross spilled the coffee he was pouring. He hadn't realized she was back.

"What's real, Dear?" he asked, grabbing a paper towel to wipe up the puddle of dark liquid.

"The house, Dad. The one in my dream. I found it all by myself," Jennifer beamed with pride.

"How could I forget?" Morgan muttered under his breath as he dumped the soggy paper towel into the garbage. For the past nine months, he and his wife had listened to Jennifer's endless detailed descriptions of the house in her dream. The big white house with a porch and an attic. The only house where she could stay, where she could be happy again.

For nearly as long, he and his wife had tried to find that house, week after week, house after house. At first, it had been exciting, but now the whole business was starting to get to him. They'd looked at more than thirty houses, but none had been right for Jennifer.

He was beginning to wonder if the house existed at all. Still, it was wonderful to have his daughter around, talking and looking happy again. So, he smiled as he turned back to her, trying to look interested.

"Where is it?" he asked. This time? he added silently.

"Well, it's a little far from here," Jennifer began, "out by Millbrook." Then her excitement took over. "But, Dad, it's amazing. It's got a huge attic, and a porch and library and apple trees and everything. Just like I dreamed."

Dreamed! Morgan thought, briefly tuning out his daughter again. Dreams is more like it. Not dreamed, as in once or twice, but dreams, as in night after night. Ever since the accident. And always the same dream, she says. About that house. A big house. White, with shutters. The friendly house, she calls it. But what if there is no friendly house? What if there is no dream? What if...?

"So, will you call her now? Dad, are you listening?" Jennifer asked impatiently.

"Yes, Dear, of course. Helen, could you come in here, please? Jennifer wants you," Morgan called out.

"Not Mom. Mrs. Jackson!" she rolled her eyes in frustration.

Mrs. Jackson was the real estate agent. She'd been showing them houses ever since they'd decided to move. But lately, Morgan thought, she seemed to be getting fed up with them.

Just last week she had said, "I've shown you every single big white house within fifty miles, Mr. Ross. I don't know where to look next. Maybe you should take a break from house-hunting for a while. Your wife seems very tired these days. Besides, you've got a lovely home already."

At that point, Morgan had stopped her.

"Not a home, Mrs. Jackson. Just a house. We must move. But, it has to be a house that's right for Jennifer."

"You said she's only eleven, Mr. Ross. I'm sure she'd get used to any house you bought." Impatience was creeping into Mrs. Jackson's voice.

"She's our only child, Mrs. Jackson." Morgan sighed. "You know how it is. We want her to be happy. That's all that ever mattered to us. So, if you'll just keep looking..."

And that's how they'd left it, with Mrs. Jackson promising to call as soon as she found something. But she hadn't sounded keen.

"What is it, Morgan?" Helen Ross asked, coming into the kitchen.

It was true. She was looking worn out lately. And pale too. No sparkle left. No get-up-and-go. But when she saw Jennifer, she perked up a little.

"Oh, you're back, Dear. Are you all right? You look..." she frowned thoughtfully, "different somehow."

"I'm so happy, Mom. And guess why? I found the friendly house at last. It's perfect."

"Do you really think so, Jennifer?"

"I know so. I went there three times. They're there, Mom. Like in the dream. I saw them."

"Jennifer wants us to call Mrs. Jackson, Helen," Morgan interrupted. "To see if the house is for sale. But I'm not so sure..."

"Do it, Morgan. We can't stay here. You know that. It's the only way."

"All right, Helen. I'll call from the den," Morgan said. "Tell me again, Jennifer, exactly where this place is so I can pin it down for Mrs. Jackson."

Five minutes later, he was back in the kitchen, and he was smiling.

"She says it's listed."

Jennifer let out a whoop.

"It's been on the market for more than four years," Morgan continued. "But she says it's in such bad shape that she never dreamed of showing it to us."

"Don't worry, Dad. It's perfect. You'll see."

Jennifer was so excited that she was flitting around the kitchen.

"Should you start packing? When do we move? Let's go."

"Calm down, Jennifer," Morgan said. "You know you have to save your energy. We'll go and see the house tomorrow."

"Tomorrow?" Helen asked.

"Mrs. Jackson is very busy today," Morgan explained. "She'll get the key tomorrow and meet us there late in the afternoon. Around six."

Millbrook was only a twenty-minute drive from Fenton, but Jennifer was so eager to show off the house that the Rosses had agreed to leave at four.

"So you can see it when it's still bright out," Jennifer had explained. "I'll show you the way when you get close."

"Maybe we could bring along some food and have a picnic first," Morgan had suggested hopefully. It had been a long time since Helen had wanted to do anything like that, and he wasn't sure what she'd say. But she had agreed, saying that it sounded like a great idea—until he'd mentioned the lake.

"We could spread out a blanket by the lake, like we used to, and..."

That's when Helen had gone pale again.

"Not the lake, Morgan," she had whispered hoarsely. "You know I can't go back there. Not since Jennifer...," her voice trailed off into silence.

"No, of course not," Morgan had said quickly, reaching out to take his wife's hand. "I wasn't thinking."

Instead, he had proposed stopping along the way for hot dogs and ice cream, and Helen had said she'd like that a lot.

And that's exactly what they'd done. But it was still only five-thirty when they turned off Highway 52 onto County Road 10.

Almost immediately, Jennifer spoke up from the back seat. "Keep your eyes on the road, Dad. It's only me. We're nearly there. See that gate up ahead on the left? Turn in there."

Morgan wheeled the car slowly down a long, tree-shaded lane.

"There it is. Isn't it beautiful?" Jennifer said softly, as the car pulled into a clearing.

"Well, it's certainly big enough," Morgan said, shutting off the ignition.

"And it was white once," Helen added dubiously, as they got out of the car.

Jennifer skipped ahead of her parents.

"Come on, you two. Hurry up. Wait till you see inside," she called from the huge porch that ran around three sides of the house. Tall, shuttered windows opened onto it from each side of the front door.

"We have to wait for Mrs. Jackson," Morgan called back. "She has the key."

"Oh, that's right. I forgot. You two need a key to get in," Jennifer giggled. Then she began to call out, "I'm here. I'm here," and drifted around the side of the house.

"All the patio furniture would fit on this porch," Morgan said, leading his wife up the steps. "What do you think, Helen?"

"What do I think? I think that Jennifer will be happy here. Listen to her, Morgan. And did you see her when she got out of the car? She was positively glowing."

At that moment, Mrs. Jackson pulled into the lane and parked.

"Sorry I'm late," she sputtered, as she grabbed her briefcase and rushed towards the porch.

"We're early," Morgan said. "And watch the steps. They need a little work."

"A little work? A lot of work, Mr. Ross. This whole place needs lots and lots of work. No one has lived here for years." Mrs. Jackson jumped back suddenly. "What's that? Did you hear that?"

"What?" Helen asked. "I didn't hear anything."

"Oh, I guess it's just me," Mrs. Jackson said. "Are you sure you want to see this place? It gives me the jitters. I can't imagine an eleven-year-old liking it. Did you finally bring Jennifer with you this time? I'd love to meet her."

I was right, Morgan thought. She is fed up with us.

Aloud, he simply said, "I told you she's uncomfortable around strangers. Now, can we go in and look around, please?"

Reluctantly, Mrs. Jackson pulled out a key, opened the door, and led the Rosses into the entrance hall.

Fifteen minutes later, she was edging back towards the hall, waiting impatiently for the Rosses to come downstairs.

Helen came out of a bedroom and waved to her from the upstairs landing.

"I just wanted to take another look at the master bedroom," she said. "We're ready now."

Morgan came out of another bedroom and, together, they walked slowly down the stairs. They were smiling.

"We'll take it, Mrs. Jackson. When can we move in?" Morgan said.

Mrs. Jackson's cheeks turned bright red. "But you haven't even asked the price yet. Mind you, that won't be a problem. It's very low—less than half what your own house is worth. But...," she hesitated.

"But what?" Helen asked.

"Look, Mrs. Ross. I'd be lying if I said I didn't want this sale. I've spent more time with you people than I have with any other clients. I mean, we've been looking for nearly nine months. But, I really don't think you should buy this house. And not just because of the state it's in."

"Why not?" asked Morgan.

Mrs. Jackson hesitated again, then continued. "This afternoon, when I stopped to pick up the key from the local real estate agent, he...," she paused.

"Go on," Helen said.

"Well, he told me something about the house." Mrs. Jackson lowered her voice. "Of course, I don't believe stuff like this myself, but he said some people think it's haunted."

"Really?" Helen said. "Tell us more."

Mrs. Jackson looked around nervously. Speaking nearly in a whisper, she continued, "Well, apparently a family used to live here, the Moranos. They had two children—a girl eleven and a boy thirteen. Five years ago, there was a terrible crash on Highway 52. Their car went off the bridge. Mr. and Mrs. Morano were saved, but not the children. They drowned. The Moranos left the house about a month later. The children had loved it out here in the country, but the house was too empty without them. It held too many memories for the parents. They just had to move."

Helen's eyes grew misty. "I know just how they felt." Then she added quickly, "How sad. It's always terrible to lose a child."

"But," Mrs. Jackson said, speaking quickly now, "people say the children aren't really lost, gone, whatever. Some say they're still here. They say they've seen them. The two of them. Playing out in the yard, and moving past the windows late at night. Some people say they've even heard them singing. Laughing too. And just last week, the agent says he saw *three* shapes at the window, not just two. Even he is starting to believe the stories."

Mrs. Jackson's cheeks were burning now. "So you see why you probably shouldn't buy this house? Besides, your daughter will hate it. She'll be scared to death of the place."

Mrs. Jackson was opening the door now, ushering the Rosses onto the porch. Then she froze.

"Did you hear that?" she croaked.

"Hear what?" Morgan asked, stepping outside.

"I thought I heard someone laughing."

"Where? Inside?" he asked.

"No, over there," Mrs. Jackson said, pointing towards a small, neglected orchard. "But there's nothing there."

Helen and Morgan looked towards the orchard. In the glow of the sunset, they could just make out the misty shapes of three children, two girls and a boy. They were darting in and out among the old apple trees as if they were playing tag.

Helen and Morgan looked back at each other and smiled.

"We'll take the house, Mrs. Jackson," they said together.

"But, your daughter. You said she didn't want all the other houses. I'm sure she'll hate this one."

"I don't think so," Morgan said. "I think she'll find it a very friendly house, don't you, Helen?"

"I know she will," Helen said. "She'll probably say it's a dream come true."

Voice from the Past

Vince was not happy. It was still light out—a warm evening in May and a Saturday to boot—and he was stuck in his room.

He punched his pillow in frustration. If he hadn't talked back to his mother at dinner, he wouldn't be in his bedroom. But he had, and she had imposed her usual sentence.

"To your room," she had ordered, "and no food, no friends, no phone calls. You obviously need time to calm down. Three hours should do it."

Three hours! She was the one who needed three hours. It had taken him all of ten minutes. He'd already forgotten what had made him so angry.

Vince flipped onto his back and stared at the ceiling. Nothing exciting there, not even a cobweb dangling. He turned to the walls. They were covered with his most prized possessions—his Detroit Tigers posters. He called the display his Tiger Zoo.

Cecil Fielder was his favorite. The huge signed picture took up nearly half of one wall. Beside it, he'd tacked a blowup of the latest team photo and arranged the rest of the posters on the other walls. He even had one of Sparky Anderson, the team's popular manager. It was signed, too.

Looking at the posters reminded him that the game had started. If his mother hadn't needed so much time to calm down, he'd be downstairs watching it on TV. Instead, he switched on his radio, hoping to catch a score.

They must be in the second inning by now, he thought, as he tried to tune in the game.

"The pitch was low and inside." The announcer's voice filled the room. "It's two and O for Fielder. Guzman winds up..."

Suddenly the voice was gone, replaced by nerve-grating, crackling static.

Vince fiddled with the dial. Static everywhere. He switched to FM. More static, and it seemed to be getting louder, even though he'd turned down the volume.

It couldn't be the batteries. He'd plugged in the adapter the night before. He got up and checked the plug and cord. Nothing wrong there.

Then he felt it—a blast of icy air. He turned to the window. It was open, but the sunset was picture perfect and the leaves on the tree outside were perfectly still. Only the curtain was moving slightly, floating as if lifted by an invisible hand.

Vince began to shiver. He sat up and pulled the comforter around his shoulders, but it didn't help much. The room was getting colder by the minute, and the static was getting louder too. Vince slipped an arm outside the comforter and hit the radio's OFF button.

The silence that followed was nearly as disturbing as the static. It was absolute. Then Vince noticed the fog. It was rolling in over the windowsill and collecting on the floor near his closet.

He jumped up and headed for the window, dragging his comforter behind him. Just as he was about to slam the window shut, he heard another noise. It was low at first, like a hoarse whisper.

Vince hesitated. The sound grew louder. As he began to pull down the window, the sound became a voice—an eerie, tortured voice that uttered an unearthly, "Nooooooooooooo."

Vince pulled back his hand and listened. Nothing.

I'm losing it, he thought, reaching for the window again. Once more, he heard it.

"Noooooooooooooooooooo."

He began to shake, and not just because he was cold. The sound seemed to be coming from near the closet. Slowly, he made himself turn towards it.

The fog had become a cloud, a gray misty cloud rising from the floor. Vince watched, spellbound, as the cloud swirled higher and began to branch out. The branches began to thicken.

Horrified, he realized what was happening. The cloud was taking a human shape.

Vince opened his mouth to yell, but no sound came out. He tried to make a dash for the door, but his feet felt rooted to the floor. It was as if he were caught in his worst nightmare.

The last wisps of fog settled around the shoulders of the horrible apparition, transforming into long, scraggly hair.

Vince found himself staring into a pair of milky white eyes. The specter was wearing a long, old-fashioned coat, thick woolly pants and brown, mud-spattered boots. A thin scarf was wrapped around its neck, but its head and hands were bare.

Slowly, it stretched out its right hand. The bony fingers beckoned to Vince and the purple-tinged lips struggled to mouth a sound.

"Commmmmmmmme."

Vince tried to yell. He had to warn his family. They had to get out of there.

"Argh!" he finally managed to shriek. "Mom, help. Help. Upstairs. Hurry."

He heard her footsteps racing up the stairs. The door swung open and there she stood, looking very worried.

"What's wrong, Vince? Did you hurt yourself?"

"Be careful, Mom. Don't come any farther. Just look, look," he pointed at the apparition. "What is it, Mom? Get me out of here, please. I can't move."

His mother raised her eyebrows and placed her hands on her hips.

"Look at what, Vince? What am I supposed to see?" she asked sharply.

"That," Vince yelled, waving his arm frantically. "There, by the closet."

His mother was angry now.

"What is this, Vince? Some kind of trick so you can get downstairs to watch the game?"

"Mom, please," Vince begged. "It's a ghost or something. Can't you see it? It's right beside you."

At this, the corners of the apparition's mouth turned up in a ghastly smile.

"Vince, this is not funny. One more stunt like this and you can forget about TV for the rest of the month. And close that window. It's cold in here."

With that, she spun around and stormed out of the room, walking straight through the specter's grotesque outstretched hand before slamming the door behind her.

Once more, the hand began to beckon.

"Commmmmmmme, you are miiinnnne," the thing wheezed, taking a shaky step towards Vince.

Vince jerked backwards. Surprised that he could move again, he wasn't prepared for what followed. His foot caught in the tangled comforter, and he crashed to the floor.

As the specter slowly drifted towards him, its arms outstretched and its face distorted in a hideous grin, he tried to untangle himself.

Suddenly, he heard his father shouting downstairs.

"Ghost? He said a ghost?"

"But, Carl, there was nothing there."

Vince heard his father's footsteps on the stairs. He was taking the steps two at a time. From the sound of it, his mother was close behind.

"Dad. Mom. Help me," he called weakly.

Dad threw open the door. He stood, his face ashen, taking in the scene. Mom, looking bewildered, was right behind him.

"Are you all right, Vince?"

"Yes," Vince croaked.

Then Dad looked directly at the apparition.

"Never!" he bellowed. "You can't have him."

Grim-faced, he gently pushed his wife to the safety of the hall. Then he turned to face the phantom.

As the sickly thing staggered closer to Vince, Dad scanned the room. Suddenly, he spotted something.

"Vince, I want you to do exactly as I tell you."

Petrified, Vince could only nod.

"Reach out slowly and get the bat."

Dad was pointing to the Louisville Slugger leaning against the wall in the corner. It had been his. Every Tiger had signed it for him back in 1964.

"Now, shove it over here. Quickly," he said.

Vince did as he was told. The creature stopped. It looked confused.

Dad snatched up the bat and looked around frantically.

"Please let this work," he muttered aloud. He grabbed a red marker from Vince's desk and scratched something on the bat. Then he gripped it with both hands and lunged straight at the ghoul. He swung wildly in all directions.

It was over in seconds. The apparition clawed the air and staggered backwards. It let out a bloodcurdling scream and began to fade.

Dad didn't stop swinging until the last icy wisp had disappeared. Then he dropped the bat and knelt beside Vince.

"He's gone. He's gone," he murmured, giving Vince a hug. "You're safe."

Mom edged into the room and joined in the hugging. Between sobs, she asked, "I couldn't see anything, Carl. What was it? What was going on?"

"I'm not sure," Dad said, "but I'll tell you what I think."

The tale he told was strange, full of fights and feuding and a tragic death more than a hundred years ago in Eastern Europe.

"Apparently, my great-great-grandfather wanted the fighting to end. As a sign of good faith, he forbade his sons to carry weapons. But old hatreds don't die easily.

"One day, two of the sons were delivering some tables and chairs to the country house of a rich merchant. Back then, my family was known for making very fine furniture. On the way through the forest, the sons were ambushed. Desperate to defend himself, one of the boys broke off a table leg and started swinging. One of the other men was killed."

"So it was self-defense, right, Dad?"

"Yes, it was. But the head of the other family wouldn't accept that. It was his sister's son who had been killed. The old man cursed my family. He said he would haunt us forever, coming back every generation to claim one male child. Because the fight had been between men, only the men would see him and only males would be claimed.

I never believed the story—until today. I always thought my grandfather made it up to scare me."

"But, Dad, how did you know what to do?"

"Well, I never believed my grandfather, but I did listen to every word. I remember him saying that the table leg the young man had used bore the family's mark."

He paused and pointed at the bat.

"The mark was a red star. I didn't know it would work, but I took a chance. What else could I do?"

Vince looked at the large red star scrawled on the bat. Then he noticed something else.

"Oh no, Dad. Look what you did."

He pointed to the signature partially blotted out by the star. "You wrecked Al Kaline's autograph. He was your favorite."

"Don't worry, Vince. Kaline was the greatest Tiger ever, and you're the greatest son. Kaline wouldn't mind. He'd say it was worth it."

Vince felt his face going red. "Thanks, Dad. You're embarrassing me."

"Then, let's get downstairs and catch the end of that game."

"Great. Oops, I almost forgot. My time isn't up. Right, Mom?"

"Well, I don't know," Mom said, pretending to look at her watch. Then she smiled and added, "That sounds like a great idea."

A Boy's Best Friend

Only one thing got Marshall through the miserable weeks after his dog, Fred, was hit by a car and killed. That was thoughts of summer camp.

Whenever memories of Fred started to get to him, he'd check the calendar over his desk and count off the days till camp was due to start.

Finally, it was the night before he was to leave for another magical summer at White Pine. Marshall picked up the picture of him and Fred that he kept on his bedside table.

"G'night, buddy," he said, as he did every night. Then he tucked it into the side pocket of his bag, right next to his three favorite Hardy Boys books.

"White Pine, here I come," he thought as he snuggled under the covers. For the first time in months, he felt really and truly happy.

But his happiness was short-lived. It lasted through the two-hour bus ride to the camp and

through the silly greetings the counselors invent-
ed for the campers. But it ended abruptly the
moment Marshall opened the door of his cabin.

There, on bed number six—right beside his—
sat Zack Vincent, perpetrator of countless Zack
Attacks. That's what the other campers called
what Zack did to his victims. Most of them had
suffered through at least one Zack Attack.

Zack worked hard at keeping his reputation as
the camp bully. Somehow, he must have sensed
that Marshall was ripe for the picking. He
launched his first attack right away.

"Well, well, well, if it isn't Sheriff. Or is it
Deputy? No, wait. Now I've got it. It's Marrrrr-
shull."

The way Zack said it, Marshall almost wished
his name were Dumbo. He walked slowly over to
his bed, trying to ignore the fact that the other
boys were watching, waiting to see what he'd do.
Harvey, a friend from last year, was the only one
who might stick up for him.

"Hey, Marrrrr-shull. Where's your badge? You
going to arrest me, Marrrrr-shull?"

Somebody should, Marshall thought, but he
said nothing. He simply went about unpacking his
bag, wishing with all his heart that his mother's
expression, "Ignore it—it'll go away" were true.

But Zack wasn't going anywhere, and he was impossible to ignore. In the next few days, he hid Marshall's sneakers, short-sheeted his bed, flipped a garter snake over top of the stall while Marshall showered, and poured water into his bed while he slept.

Marshall woke embarrassed, convinced he'd wet his bed. It was only later, when he overheard Zack bragging about it, that he realized what had happened. He was living a nightmare and there was no end in sight.

That night after dinner, Marshall asked to be excused from campfire. It was the first time he'd done it, so the counselors gave him permission.

Thankful for some time to himself, Marshall got ready for bed and scrunched down under the covers with his flashlight, a Hardy Boys book and his picture of Fred. He'd been using it as a bookmark all through camp. That way he could sneak a peek at it as often as he wanted.

Harvey had asked about Fred. Harvey had a dog, too—Bowser. The previous summer, he and Marshall had spent a lot of time swapping dog stories.

This summer, though, there was no more dog talk. Harvey didn't want to hurt Marshall's feelings by going on about how great Bowser was. And Marshall didn't dare talk about Fred for fear he'd start to cry. Zack would have a field day if he ever caught Marshall bawling like a baby.

Fred and Zack. The two had become woven together in Marshall's mind. The more Zack tormented him, the more he longed to have Fred back.

He stared at Fred's picture, wishing he could make him materialize. Then it wouldn't matter what Zack did to him.

Fred and Zack. Zack and Fred. Marshall forced his eyes to stay open just long enough so he could switch off his flashlight and stuff his book—and bookmark—under his pillow. Then he curled up on his side, his back to Zack's bed, and fell asleep.

It was still dark when Marshall woke up, covered in sweat and shaking like Jello. The nightmare again. The one that had haunted him ever since camp started.

In it, Marshall stood over Zack, watching him choke on a peanut butter sandwich. Fred was there too, yapping and biting at Zack's ankles. As Zack writhed helplessly on the cabin floor, Marshall felt himself starting to laugh—a loud, gloating cackle that turned his blood to ice. As Zack gasped and held out his hands for help, Marshall turned his back and walked towards the door.

But the door was covered by an enormous piece of paper. On it, scrawled in huge letters, was a

Chinese proverb: he who seeks revenge should dig two graves. Marshall had seen it before—in English class when his teacher used it to introduce a story about a man trying to get even with a friend who had betrayed him.

The paper swayed, blocking Marshall's exit. Still laughing horribly, he tore through it and pushed his way outside.

For a moment, he felt himself floating. In the dark below were two freshly dug graves. Zack's lifeless body lay in one. Then he started to fall.

That's when he always woke up. Every night. Right on cue. His arms flailing, struggling to stop himself from falling into the second grave.

The cabin was quiet, except for the rhythmic buzz of Harvey's snoring. As his eyes adjusted to the darkness, Marshall could just make out Zack, lying on his side, facing him. Zack was sound asleep, a smile creasing the corners of his mouth.

He's probably dreaming about what he's going to do to me tomorrow, Marshall thought. I wish he'd disappear. And, most of all, I wish you were here, Fred. I'd sic you on that creep. You'd teach him a thing or two. Geez, I miss you, little buddy.

Marshall eventually fell asleep again, his eyes moist with secret, silent tears.

Things got worse the next morning. His tossing and turning during the night must have knocked his book to the floor. He woke up to find Zack waving Fred's picture in front of his eyes.

"So, who's this, Marrrrr-shull? Your girlfriend? Hey, guys, Marshall's girlfriend is a real dog." Zack laughed mockingly. Some of the other kids joined in weakly.

"Give it back," Marshall said, trying to get up.

Zack leaned over and shoved the picture into Marshall's face.

"Give it back," Marshall mumbled.

Zack didn't budge. Suddenly Marshall pulled back both legs and kicked with all his might. Zack tumbled to the floor. Marshall followed, in a tangle of sheets and blankets.

"Give it to me, Zack. Right now. It's mine."

Zack scrambled to his feet and moved to the other side of the bunk.

"Marshall's girlfriend's a dog. Marshall's girl-friend's a dog," he taunted.

Marshall struggled to stand up. As he got to his feet, he tripped on the sheet and fell across Zack's bed. Desperately, he grabbed for the picture.

"You want it?" Zack jeered. "Here, have it." He ripped the photo apart, crumpled the pieces, and tossed them at Marshall. Then he turned and headed for the door.

Marshall picked up the pieces and stood up. Fighting back tears, he yelled, "You'll be sorry for this, Zack. You wait. You're nothing but a bully. That's all. A scummy, scuzzy, brainless bully!"

Someone gasped. Then there was dead silence in the cabin. Shocked, everyone was quiet, including Marshall.

Slowly, Zack swung around and glared at him. Then, as if deciding that he'd done enough damage, he turned and strolled out the door.

Marshall tried to salvage the photograph. He spread out the pieces on his bunk, hoping he'd be able to tape them back together. It was no use. A tear ran through the middle of Fred's face and white cracks showed where Zack had crumpled the pieces. The picture was ruined. Fred was gone, and now so was his picture.

Thoughts of Fred and what Zack had done weighed heavily on Marshall as he trudged to the dining hall for breakfast. He didn't dare line up at the steam table for scrambled eggs and sausages. That was a favorite place for Zack to carry out a sneak attack on his victims.

Instead, he went directly to his cabin's table where there was a supply of toast, cereal and juice. Before he sat down beside Harvey, he checked his chair to make sure Zack hadn't painted it with jam.

As if reading his mind, Harvey said, "Don't worry. He's not here."

"Where is he?" Marshall asked.

"Gone to have a shower," Harvey said, breaking into a grin. "He never made it to breakfast. He tripped and fell into the only mud puddle for miles around. Even some of the counselors laughed."

"You're kidding."

"Nope. It was great. You should have been there."

Marshall was there the next time Zack tripped, on the way to lunch. And he was there when Zack tripped on the way to the dock too. He had his bathing suit on and skinned his knees badly.

Then he tripped on the way to campfire, letting out an agonized yell as he tumbled to his battered knees again. This time, Marshall actually winced in sympathy.

That night, Zack went to bed without tormenting anyone, not even Marshall. Marshall fell asleep smiling. At last Zack was getting exactly what he deserved.

For the first time since camp started, Marshall slept peacefully and woke feeling refreshed. Zack, however, woke up grumpy as a rattlesnake, complaining that he'd nearly frozen to death.

"...and whoever kept pulling off the covers better watch out," he threatened. "When I catch him, he'll wish he'd never been born."

He glared straight at Marshall as he said this. Then he snatched his blankets off the floor and began to make his bed.

Marshall made his own bed quickly, anxious to get as far from Zack as possible. In a mood like that, there was no telling what he might do.

Mind you, Marshall thought, losing your blankets like that could be really irritating, especially on a cool night. He remembered how Fred sometimes used to pull off his covers. He hated waking up chilled to the bone.

That day, strange things continued to happen to Zack. In the morning, he fell backwards off the dock, claiming a horsefly had taken a huge chunk out of his ankle. But when the waterfront director offered him After-Byte to rub on the spot, Zack could find no sign of swelling or redness anywhere.

At dinner—a wiener roast around the fire— Zack claimed that someone snatched his hot dog. Even though he'd cooked and drowned it in ketchup himself, he was convinced that someone had tied a string to it and yanked it away.

When the counselors told him to lighten up, he flew into a rage and stormed off. He was lying in bed, his face pressed into his pillow, when the others returned.

The next morning, the cabin woke to more of Zack's ranting.

"If I catch that dog, I'll stuff him in a sack with a big rock and heave him into the lake."

"What dog?" Harvey asked.

"The one that yapped outside all night."

"I didn't hear any dog," Harvey said. "Did you guys?"

The others, Marshall included, shook their heads, mystified.

"What do you mean, you didn't hear it? Are you deaf? Yap, yap, yap—all night long. I'm going to set a bear trap out there tonight."

Zack's talk of a yapping dog reminded Marshall of Fred. Fred used to do that sometimes—yap, yap, yap, until he got what he wanted. Wait a minute, Marshall thought. Fred used to pull the covers off my bed, too. And snatch food at barbecues. That was one of his favorite tricks.

Suddenly, there was a loud crash followed by a scream. Zack lay sprawled at the bottom of the cabin steps. He was crying.

Giggles rippled through the cabin. The mighty Attacker was blubbering like a baby.

Someone called out "Wacko Zacko" and the giggles turned to hoots of mocking laughter. Everyone was laughing. Everyone except Harvey, who never laughed at other people's troubles—and Marshall.

Marshall wasn't laughing because he'd just added another item to his mental list. Fred was always underfoot. It seemed like someone was forever tripping over him. This is impossible, Marshall thought. It can't be. Fred is...

Zack screamed again. Harvey and Raj, who were trying to help him up, jumped back.

"My leg," Zack moaned, collapsing against Harvey. "I can't stand up. Get help. I think it's broken."

Marshall ran and collected two counselors who used a firefighter's lift to carry Zack to the infirmary. Marshall and the others trailed behind, then hung around outside waiting for word on Zack's injury.

Finally, the nurse emerged to announce that Zack's leg wasn't broken, but it was badly sprained.

"He'll be spending the next couple of days in the infirmary," he said.

The rest of the day was great. With Zack safely out of commission, everyone relaxed. Everyone except Marshall. He struggled to come up with an explanation for what was happening. Every time, he got the same impossible answer—Fred.

Later that evening, when the other kids were changing into their bathing suits for a midnight swim, Marshall slipped off to the infirmary. Quietly, he skulked around it. Then, he stood statue-

still under the window and listened intently. He saw and heard nothing unusual.

Finally, he crouched in the darkness and whispered, "Fred, Fred. Here boy. C'mere, boy."

Nothing. Nevertheless, he went on.

"Listen to me, boy. I think you're out there. If you are, thanks. You really came through. But, Fred, it's over now, okay? I can't stand to see Zack feeling like I did. Give the guy a break, Fred. He's got no friends. I'm okay now, fellah. Really, I am."

As Marshall stood up to leave, he stepped on a stick. It snapped with a loud crack.

"Who's there?" Zack called out sharply. Fear filled his voice. "Is that you, dog?"

Marshall wavered. Should I answer—or just get out of here? He sounds really scared.

"It's me, Zack. Marshall."

"What are you doing out there?" Some of the bravado was returning to Zack's voice.

"Oh...I just came by to say good night."

"Yeah?" Zack sounded surprised.

"Yeah," Marshall said, pushing open the door. In the glow of a night light, Marshall could just see Zack's head poking out from under the covers.

"Shhh," Zack whispered. "The nurse might not be asleep yet. He just finished putting ice on my ankle a while ago."

"How's the leg?" Marshall whispered back.

"It hurts."

"Sorry."

"So am I."

Marshall couldn't believe his ears. "What did you say?" he asked.

"I said, 'So am I.'" Zack looked like he was bracing for Marshall to say something mean.

Marshall stared. Then he said softly, "It's okay."

Zack let out his breath and his face softened. "Thanks," he said.

"No problem. See you in the morning?"

"Sure."

Marshall tiptoed back to his cabin and slipped into bed. By the time the others got back from their swim, he was sound asleep. He dreamed that Fred was curled up at the foot of his bed.

After breakfast, Marshall returned to the infirmary. Zack was sitting up, eating breakfast.

"How's the leg?" Marshall asked.

"Much better, thanks."

"Great," said Marshall. "Does it still hurt?"

"Not too much. I think the nurse must have put a heating pad on it in the night. I remember waking up and thinking how good it felt to have something soft and warm tucked around my ankle."

Marshall looked at the foot of the bed, then at Zack. Smiling, he said, "Yeah, I know just what you mean."

Robber's Reward

T he day started like any other. Jose's mother, a lab technician, left for the hospital around seven-thirty. His dad wasn't home yet from another night of driving cab. Jose and his sister fought over the bathroom and, as usual, he lost.

Finally, Maria headed off to school—her classes started at eight-thirty—and Jose had a few minutes to himself. He flicked on the TV and began to crunch his way through a bowl of corn flakes.

The news was on—not exactly prime time viewing. His thoughts wandered to the science fair topic he'd decided on last night. For once, he'd picked something he was really interested in.

He wanted to know why the shower curtain moved in and wrapped itself around him when he turned on the water. So did Maria. She always screamed "soap scum attack" when it happened to her.

His mom said a lot of science could be learned by answering this question, and she was pretty smart about math and science. He wasn't so sure about his teacher, though. And she was the one who needed to give the green light to his topic this morning.

"...and police are still at the scene of the bank break-in at Fifth and Cleveland..."

Fifth and Cleveland! That was just three blocks away. Jose passed that corner every morning on the way to school. He suddenly tuned in to the newscaster's words.

"Reports are still sketchy, but it looks as if the alarm may have interrupted a burglary in progress. The first officers on the scene found a man, believed to be one of the robbers, dead in front of the vault. Sergeant Coleman of the MPD refused to speculate about how the man died. He would say only that it's clear the dead man had not been alone in the bank. Police are asking people to avoid that intersection until..."

Jose jumped up from the table. He switched off the TV, dumped his bowl in the sink and tore into his bedroom. He grabbed his knapsack, stopped off at the bathroom to give his teeth a two-second brush, and dashed out of the apartment.

A large crowd was gathered in front of the bank when Jose got there. He jostled his way through the people until he was stopped by a thick, yellow plastic ribbon that warned, Police Line—Do Not Cross.

Jose was fascinated. An ambulance, its red lights flashing, was parked near the door of the bank. Police cars and equipment vans emblazoned with the logos of the city's TV stations were everywhere. Reporters and camera crews were scurrying about, and police officers were questioning people on the street and controlling the parade of individuals moving into and out of the bank.

Through the bank's double entrance doors, Jose could just make out a small circle of people hovering over something on the floor. That must be where the body is, he thought. They never move it until they've looked for all the evidence. He knew that. It always happened that way on TV.

Suddenly, police officers moved to the doors and held them open as two uniformed paramedics began to walk slowly forward. Jose realized what was happening. They were bringing out the body.

The crowd grew silent as the paramedics emerged and loaded the stretcher carefully into the ambulance. Jose stared. It was exciting, but it bothered him too. Someone had died. Somebody's brother, husband or even father.

"Husband *and* father," he heard a voice say.

"Huh?" Jose swung around to see who'd spoken. No one was paying any attention to him. He turned back, feeling foolish. For a second, he could have sworn someone had read his mind.

"I did. Weird, isn't it?" he heard the voice again.

Jose spun around. Again, no one was even looking his way. The crowd was thinning now. The person closest to him—an older woman—was several feet away. But the voice, a low, throaty whisper, had sounded as if it were right at his ear. It was a man's voice.

"I'm right here, kid."

Jose shivered. This is spooky, he thought. He'd heard voices once before, at summer camp. But that had been Charlie McKenzie up to his usual tricks. He loved to wait until someone was asleep, then whisper dirty jokes in his ear. Charlie wasn't anywhere around. In fact, right now, Charlie was probably at school, waiting for the bell to ring.

And that's where I should be too, Jose decided. His mother always said his imagination worked overtime. Too much television, she'd say. It does things to your brain. Jose backed away from the yellow tape and started to jog along Fifth Street towards the school.

"Slow down, kid. I'm new at this."

The voice was following him. He was sure of it now. Terrified, Jose began to run.

"Wait. This is using up too much energy."

Jose felt a tugging at his back. He stopped and whipped around. Nothing. There was nothing there. He was petrified, too scared to move. He stood rooted to the spot, his knees knocking and his stomach churning.

"Sorry, kid. But it worked. You stopped. Now will you listen to me, please?"

Jose detected a note of desperation in the voice. Stay or go? School was just two blocks away. Go to school. You'll be safe there, he thought.

"Maybe not. I haven't gone through any walls yet, but I'm willing to try. Besides, there's always a window."

"All right, all right," Jose muttered, trying not to move his lips. He looked around to see if anyone had heard. He didn't want any of the other kids to see him talking to himself. Luckily, the coast was clear, for the moment.

He ducked up an alley and stammered, "Who...whoever or...whatever you are...what do you want from me?"

I can't believe I'm doing this, he thought. I'm talking to it, whatever *it* is. Am I crazy or what?

"You're not crazy. But I was. Now I'm dead. And I shouldn't be, you know."

Suddenly, the metal lid from a battered garbage can clattered to the pavement next to him. Jose jumped as the sound echoed up and down the alley. Then he heard rustling in the can. He stood perfectly still. More rustling, and some scratching. Jose stopped breathing. More scratching. His imagination shifted into high gear. What sort of specter was about to materialize?

When a scraggly tabby cat poked its face over the top of the can and blinked at him, Jose let out a long, slow sigh of relief. The cat jumped lightly to the ground and ran off. Jose was tempted to follow. Instead, he looked around one more time to make sure he was alone.

Alone? That's funny, he thought. I wish I really were alone. Then it hit him. Whatever it was, it had figured out what he was thinking. He hated the idea of someone being in his head like that. But it would take care of the problem of getting caught talking out loud to empty space.

What are you? Jose thought. What do you want from me?

Silence. He concentrated harder. What do you want? Not a sound. It's gone! Or I'm sane again, he thought. This might be his chance to escape. He turned to leave.

"Stop, please. Don't go." The voice was coming from his right, over by the wall.

Jose's fear returned. He shut his eyes and concentrated even harder. What do you want?

"Please, say something. Say you'll help."

"Why do I have to say something?" Jose whispered. "You know what I'm thinking."

"I can't seem to do that anymore. It started when they loaded me onto to the stretcher. I knew what the cops were thinking. Then, when they wheeled me out to the ambulance, all sorts of thoughts came flooding in. All those people. It was rough. That crowd was pretty hostile. Some ugly thoughts out there. Except for you. You thought about my family."

The voice paused briefly. Jose thought he heard a sob. Then the voice went on.

"That's why I picked you. But I can't read your mind anymore. In fact, I don't know how much time I have left. Everything is starting to feel different. Will you help me?"

The impact of what he'd just heard hit Jose in the stomach like a baseball bat.

"You're the...," Jose gulped. "You're the... uh...man at the bank?"

"The dead guy. Yeah."

Jose gasped. "Right, then," he sputtered, trying to sound calm. "I have to go now. I'm going to get it. I'm really late for school."

"Don't go. Not yet. I have to set the record straight. You've got to help me do that. Please, for my boy's sake," the voice pleaded.

"But why should I help you? You're a..."

"A crook? A bank robber? Say it, kid. It's true. I know it was really stupid, but I needed the money and...well...I let my friend talk me into it. But it was the first time. Really. You've got to believe me."

"I don't know what to believe anymore."

"I know how you feel. But listen, please. First, my name's Jim. Jim Robertson. And you're...?"

"Jose." Jose hesitated. Last names made it easier for someone to find you. Then he realized how ridiculous that thought was. This thing, this spirit, this ghost could probably find him anywhere, anytime.

"Ramirez," he added. "Jose Ramirez." There. I've done it. I just introduced myself to a ghost.

"Pleased to meet you, Jose. I'm telling the truth. It really was the first time. It's no excuse, I know, but things were bad. I'd lost my job. The rent was overdue and the landlord was threatening to throw us—me, my wife and son—out of our apartment.

"So Harry—my best friend, Harry—came up with this plan. Nothing to it, the lying scumbag said. He used to work at the bank as a security guard. I know the layout, he said. No one'll get hurt. Ha. What a joke!"

"So what went wrong?" Jose was surprised to find himself interested.

"Nothing, at first. Everything went like clock-work until…"

Suddenly, everything became clear to Jose. "Until he tricked you," he blurted. "When he didn't need you anymore, he killed you, right, and took the money for himself?"

"That's right. And now Harry'll get away with the money—and with murder. My murder. And the truth will never come out. Not that it's so pretty. But, if the cops get Harry, maybe my wife will understand a little better. Maybe she'll be able to explain things to the boy when he's bigger. I'm not all bad, you know."

The voice trailed off at that point. Jose had a minute to think. I'm already in big trouble. School started half an hour ago. And not even the most gullible teacher will believe this story.

Aloud, he said, "Okay, what can I do?"

"Thanks, kid," the voice sounded relieved, but tired. It seemed to be growing fainter.

"Here's what you can do. There's this crime tip number…"

"I know. It's 577-…"

"Good, you know it. We'll go to that pay phone over there. If you dial the number for me, I'll tell them what happened at the bank. They won't know it's me. They'll just think I'm a sleazeball turning in a friend. And they'll be right, won't they? I'll give them my good, old friend, Harry."

"That's it? That's all you want?"

"That's it. If I could do it myself, I would."

"Okay, let's go then," Jose said, reaching into his pocket for a quarter.

Jose dialed the number and kept the receiver to his ear as a deep voice answered, "Officer Greenbloom. Thank you for calling Crime Tips."

Jose could almost feel Jim leaning beside him. Shivers rippled down his spine.

"Hello," Jim said, "I know what happened at..."

"Hello?" Greenbloom repeated. "Is anybody there?"

Jose held out the phone a little farther, trying to figure out how to make it easier for Jim to speak into the receiver.

"I'm here," Jim spoke up. "A man named Harry..."

"Is anyone there? Hello?" Greenbloom said loudly.

"He can't hear me, kid! He can't hear me," Jim said, panic in his voice. "What'll I do? Can you hear me? Am I gone?"

"I hear you," Jose said, covering the mouthpiece. "But maybe I'm the only one who can."

"Oh no," Jim moaned.

Jose looked at the receiver in his hand. He swallowed hard and put the phone back to his ear.

"I'm sorry," he began nervously. "I dropped the phone."

Shakily, he told the officer what he'd learned. Jim helped, whispering the answers to the officer's questions. Jose even managed to work in information about where Harry planned to hide the money—in a locker at the bus terminal.

He could almost feel Jim nodding enthusiastically when he added that if the police staked out the terminal, they could probably catch Harry red-handed when he went to pick up the money.

But when Greenbloom asked how to get the reward to him if the tip led to an arrest, Jose panicked. He covered the mouthpiece.

"Go for it," Jim whispered hoarsely. "You earned it. You don't have to give your name. They'll work out something with you."

Jose was tempted. Crime Tips paid $1,000 if an arrest was made. But somehow it didn't seem right to take it, and he wasn't sure why.

"Just a minute, please," he said, and covered the mouthpiece again.

"Jim, what's your wife's name?"

"Maria," Jim answered faintly.

"And your address?"

"394 West 15th. Apartment 1B. Why?"

Jose spoke quickly into the phone, "The reward goes to Maria Robertson, 394 West 15th, Apartment 1B."

"But," sputtered the voice at the other end of the line. "That's the name and address of..."

Jose hung up and slumped against the wall of the phone booth. His knees were trembling.

Weakly, Jim said, "Thanks, Jose. You're something else. Your folks must be really proud of you."

At the mention of his folks, Jose panicked and pushed his way out of the phone booth.

"Well, they won't be if the school called already to find out why I'm not there. I've really gotta go."

"So do I, kid. I think my time's nearly up."

"Oh, well...good luck."

What an unbelievably dumb thing to say! Jose thought. Then he started to run. There'd be time to think later, after he got to school.

By the time he reached his home room, Jose had decided to go with a version of the truth. As Ms. Falconi glared at him, he explained that he'd stopped to watch what was going on at the bank and lost track of time.

Ms. Falconi lectured him on the evils of lateness, then leveled a parting shot, "And I suppose you also lost track of your science fair topic."

"No, I've got that."

"Well, what is it? How to investigate bank robberies in three easy lessons?" Some of the kids giggled.

"No...it's to find out why the curtain moves in towards you when you turn on the shower."

That started even more giggles.

"What did you say? You're on thin ice already, Mr. Ramirez. This is no time for joking."

"I'm not joking, Ms. Falconi."

Jose heard a faint whisper near his ear.

"The window, kid. Look. Hurry."

Oh no, Jose thought. I can't take this.

"Hurry, kid. I haven't got much more time."

Jose looked at the open windows that lined the wall of the classroom. Shapeless blue drapes hung limply over them. Suddenly, a single pair of drapes swayed slightly, then pressed against the open window, as if they were being sucked outside.

"There, like that," Jose pointed at the window.

"Yeah, why does that happen?" Charlie McKenzie yelled.

"I guess Jose will find out and tell us," Ms. Falconi said. "I wonder why it happened at only one window."

"Probably just a fluke breeze," Jose offered.

Thanks, Jim, he thought, watching the drapes fall back into place. Once again, like the air outside, they were perfectly still.

Wall-to-Wall Horror

F rom the day we moved into the old house on Hill Street, I felt like someone was watching us. It was nothing I could pin down. Just a feeling that came over me every now and then, especially when I was alone.

Sometimes, it happened while I was watching TV in the living room. Suddenly, I'd think my older brother, Phil, was trying to sneak up and scare me, a favorite trick of his. I'd whip around to catch him—only he wouldn't be there.

I never mentioned it to anybody. For sure, Mom and Dad would think I was going nuts—and I might have agreed. When I got the creepy-crawly feeling, I just tried to ignore it.

This got a lot harder, though, after Dad laid the new carpet in the den off the living room.

The den was a nice little room. Mom and Dad had furnished it with a rocking chair and an over-stuffed couch they'd picked up at a garage sale. Dad built some shelves beside the small fireplace and Mom rewired an old lamp.

All in all, it was a cozy place, perfect for curling up with a good book. Except that I couldn't stay in the room for more than a few minutes. The feeling that someone was watching me was just too strong.

I wasn't the only one who was uncomfortable in there, either. It seemed like nobody ever stayed in the den for long. Mom blamed it on the carpet.

"I've tried three times to get rid of that disgusting stain right in the middle. It just won't come out," she said.

She got no argument from Dad. "A real amateur laid this carpet," he said. "It doesn't lie flat, it's buckling in the corners, and whoever did it never bothered to nail down the loose floorboards beforehand. See where it's wearing out over those two ridges? Loose boards under there."

We didn't have much money to fix up the house—and it needed a lot of work. That's why we'd been able to afford it in the first place.

We knew that fixing it up was going to take a long time, and we'd all have to pitch in. Well, Phil and I would have to pitch in. Brian, who was four, and Sally, who was one-and-a-half, were too young to do much but get in the way.

There was lots to do, but replacing the ugly carpet in the den quickly moved to number one on everybody's fix-it list.

Mom found a nice rose-colored remnant that was nearly the right size and Dad trimmed and installed it in less than an hour. He'd been right about the loose floor boards. He nailed down four of them before laying the foam underpad.

When we moved the furniture back into the room, everyone agreed that it looked great. The first thing I did was bring down some of my library books to add to the collection on the shelves beside the fireplace. I could hardly wait to curl up on the couch with *Eyes of the Dragon*. Surely now that the room looked so nice, it would feel nice too.

How wrong I was. I lasted ten minutes. Then I couldn't stand it any longer. It felt as if every knot in the pine paneling was an eye, staring right at me.

The next afternoon, I tried again. No sooner had I settled down on the couch than the rocking chair started swaying gently back and forth—all by itself! I headed for the living room, trying to convince myself that it must have been the wind.

The next morning—Saturday—I slept late. I was still rubbing sleep out of my eyes when I started to wander downstairs around ten o'clock.

That's when I heard Mom yell, "Oh no!"

I flew down the last few steps and raced into the living room. She was standing in the doorway to the den.

"Look," she said, pointing to the carpet.

"Geez," I said. The stain was back. Not as dark and not as big. But definitely there.

By this time, Dad and Phil had arrived on the scene, too.

Mom asked Dad if he'd noticed anything wrong with the boards when he was nailing them down.

"Nope. They were just fine. Not oily or stained or anything. Just a little chipped along the edges in some places, that's all. A few rough edges wouldn't do that," he said, pointing to the stain.

He looked puzzled. Then he turned to Phil, with one of those "Ah-ha, I've got it" looks in his eyes.

"Okay, Phil. Time's up. Not a bad trick. But it's time to confess. What is it, water? I'll have your head if you used something that will leave a mark."

"I didn't do anything, Dad," Phil protested.

"It's not damp, Ron," Mom said. "I felt it."

"You then?" Dad said, looking straight at me.

"Dad, this is not my style. Besides, thanks to my dear brother here, I know what it's like to be on the receiving end of a joke like this."

As I spoke, I watched Phil's face. He looked as baffled as I was. I was pretty sure he wasn't the culprit—but, if he wasn't, who was?

Mom decided that she wasn't going to spend the rest of the weekend scrubbing a rug.

"I'll rent a steam cleaner next week and do the bedrooms at the same time."

Even then, I had a feeling that steam cleaning wasn't likely to be the answer. And when I thought about it some more, I was sure.

By Sunday night, I knew I'd need Phil's help. After dinner, I called him into the den. The rest of the family was in the living room watching Disney on TV.

"Look, can you see it?" I whispered, pointing to the rocking chair.

"That's weird. It's moving."

"Keep your voice down. But you can see it too?"

He nodded.

"That's a relief. I was beginning to think I was in big trouble up here." I tapped my head.

"Now look here," I whispered, pointing to the stain on the carpet. "It's growing, Phil. Take my word for it. And look here. The boards have lifted again."

"What is this, Lizzie—*The Twilight Zone* or something? We better tell Mom and Dad."

"No!" I said sharply, grabbing his arm. "I'm not finished. Listen, Phil...," I swallowed hard, "have you felt anything...odd...since we moved in here?"

He looked at me strangely.

"Like someone's watching you?" I added quickly. "Come on, Phil, the truth."

He took a deep breath, then let it out slowly. "A few times, yes. But there's nothing here, Lizzie. I've checked—lots."

"Why didn't you say anything?"

"And let you think I was a wimp—or that I was losing my marbles. Get serious!"

I grimaced. "I know exactly what you mean. I don't think Mom and Dad have noticed a thing. You know what they're like. They would have found a way to ask us without letting on that anything was wrong. I haven't picked up on anything like that, have you?"

He shook his head.

"Okay, so let's suppose they haven't noticed. Think about it, Phil. If we say something, it'll take forever to get them to believe us."

"So, what do you suggest?" Phil asked.

"Well, it's not as if anything really bad has happened. Whatever it is, I don't think it's trying to hurt us."

"I guess not." Phil didn't sound totally convinced.

"So, I think it's trying to tell us something."

Phil rolled his eyes and snorted, but I hurried on before he could interrupt.

"Just listen, okay? If we could figure out what it's trying to tell us, then maybe it would go away."

Suddenly, the rocking chair started moving again, more quickly this time. I grabbed Phil's hand and held on tight.

"See, I'm telling you, Phil," I said urgently. "It's giving us a sign that we're on the right track."

"I don't know, Liz." Phil still wasn't totally with me.

Before he could finish, though, my library books—no others, just mine—tumbled off the shelf, landing on the floor with a loud thump.

Phil stared at the messy pile, then shrugged.

"All right. I believe, I believe. What do you want to do?"

The first thing I wanted to do was go upstairs. Now that my thoughts were actually in words, my skin was starting to crawl. I wanted out of that room.

Upstairs, I suggested that Phil pump his new friend, Terrance, for information about the people who had lived in the house before us.

"Ask him at school tomorrow, okay?"

The real estate agent had told us only that the owner had died of a heart attack and that a nephew in New York—his only relative—had arranged the sale through a lawyer. Terrance had lived three houses away all his life, so he should know more than that.

"All right, I'll do it...but why?"

"Well," I began, trying to sound more confident than I felt, "because that's a good a place to start. In lots of the stories I've read, a ghost—if that's what this is—hangs around because it has unfinished business of some sort."

I'd read piles of ghost stories, so I knew what I was talking about. I'd even done an English project on a horror theme. But this was not a time for reading. This was a time for doing something about what might be a genuine horror story—with us as the main characters.

The next evening, at dinner, I had the strangest sensation. It felt as if something were hovering over us, like a cloud. But when I looked up at the ceiling, all I saw were a few cracks in the plaster. I was still staring at them when I realized Dad was talking to me.

"Earth to Lizzie."

"Oh, sorry. I wasn't paying attention."

"No kidding. I was just asking what you've been reading lately."

Dad was like that. He tried to ask each of us kids—even Sally—a question at dinner. He said it was to keep the fine art of conversation alive.

"Are you still on that horror kick, or have you moved on to other things?"

"I guess I'm sort of still on it, but not so much. Right now, I'm reading a long, modern fairy tale."

"Well, as long as you don't start believing in those ghosts and monsters..."

Dad never finished his sentence. Suddenly, he was on his feet, trying to shake off the hot coffee that had spilled into his lap.

Mom, Phil and I all jumped up at the same time, grabbing for the paper towels to wipe up the mess.

"Sorry about that," Dad said when things settled down. "I must have bumped it with my elbow."

I knew he hadn't, though. His elbow had been nowhere near his coffee mug. I sneaked another peek at the ceiling. Nothing there. My hand shook as I finished my milk.

After we did the dishes, Mom and Dad took Brian and Sally to Grandma's for a visit. I just hung around the house feeling nervous.

Finally, I heard Phil come in from basketball practice. I was dying to hear what he'd found out from Terrance. I raced down to the kitchen and sat at the table across from him while he wolfed down some warmed-over stew.

"So?" I said expectantly.

"You may be on to something," he said between mouthfuls. "I hate to think what, though."

"So, tell me. Tell me."

"Their name was Patterson. And it's true. Mr. Patterson died of a heart attack, like the agent said. But he'd been acting strange for a long time before that. Talking to himself, keeping all the lights on all night. Sometimes, he'd open the door and start yelling stuff like, 'Keep away. Leave me alone,' when no one was there. Everybody said he went crazy after his wife was declared dead."

"Declared dead? What do you mean?"

"Terrance says she was reported missing about ten years ago. Just disappeared one day. He remembers hearing his mother tell someone that she probably left because Mr. Patterson was so grumpy all the time. The police searched all over and her picture was on TV too. But they never found a trace of her—or her body. Finally, Mr. Patterson applied to have her declared dead. Everybody said it was so he could collect the insurance."

My stomach felt like it had hit the floor. I looked at Phil. "Are you thinking what I'm thinking?"

"Don't say it," Phil answered grimly. "Maybe it's not that. Maybe he just hid something of hers in there and she wants us to have it."

"And maybe I'm really Madonna," I said. "Seriously, Phil...what should we do?"

Phil put down his empty milk glass and leaned back. "Well, we could forget all about it and..."

We both watched, horrified, as his glass tipped over and started to roll across the table. I grabbed it as it reached the edge and carefully set it upright.

Then, I looked at Phil.

"I don't think that's an option," I said. Goose bumps had begun to spread up my legs and arms.

He nodded. "Well then," he said, "we could tell Mom and Dad that we think there's a...ghost...under the carpet in the den."

We both stared at the glass. It began to rock back and forth.

"Yeah," I said quickly, "we could do that. But they'll never take us seriously. Maybe we should just check it out ourselves. "

Again, we both zeroed in on the glass. It quit moving and sat perfectly still, just like a glass is supposed to.

Now I was sure I was on the right track.

"Look, Phil." I was getting pretty excited. The words just came tumbling out. "You know how Grandma hates us to leave when we visit. Mom and Dad won't be home for hours."

"So?" Phil eyed me suspiciously.

"So, it's the best chance we're likely to get for a while. Let's just do it!"

Phil looked at me hard, the way he does when I surprise him. "You're serious, aren't you?"

"You scared?" I asked. I stopped talking and waited. I know how to deal with Phil. He stared at the floor, his face twisted into a thoughtful frown.

Suddenly, he pushed back his chair and stood up. "Okay, let's go. We better do it right now 'cause if I think about it for five minutes, I'm going to decide that we're both crazy."

As we grabbed the rocking chair and carried it into the living room, Phil said, "You know there's no basement under this wing of the house, Liz. There might be nothing under here but dirt."

"We'll know soon enough, then, won't we?" I said, heading back into the den.

In ten minutes, the room was empty except for the new carpet.

Phil and I got to work with a crowbar and a claw hammer. Once we'd rolled up the carpet, the floor boards lay exposed.

"See?" I said, pointing to the boards that had lifted again. "See how they're loose. Dad really nailed them down, too."

My voice echoed in the empty room. With every step we took, the floor creaked. A little light came in from the living room, but most of the den was in shadow.

Phil wedged the crowbar under one of the loose boards and leaned on it. I grabbed the hammer and pitched in. As we pried the nails out of the old dry timber, they seemed to groan.

Phil was breathing hard and I'd broken into a sweat by the time we'd freed all four of the loose boards. We knelt beside them, reluctant to take the next step.

Phil's voice trembled a little as he said, "Liz, we don't have to do this, you know."

I looked at him, my heart pounding. "Yes, we do."

Phil just nodded.

My hands shook as we lifted the boards and laid them aside. We stood at opposite ends of the long rectangular hole we'd made in the floor, staring into blackness.

"Wh... what do you see?" I couldn't believe my voice sounded so small.

"Nothing," said Phil, "it's too dark down there. Hand me the flashlight."

I couldn't believe what I said next. "No way. This was my idea."

I knelt beside the hole, peered in and flipped the switch on the flashlight. Two inches from my nose, a skeletal finger reached toward me.

I screamed and jumped to my feet. Phil had been leaning over my shoulder and we both fell in a tangled heap. The flashlight rolled across the floor and came to rest at the edge of the hole.

The thin beam of light revealed a skeleton. Its right hand lay across its chest, palm up, as if it had been pushing against the floorboards.

Everything happened pretty fast after that. Mom and Dad came home to find police cars in the driveway. Lieutenant Volpe from the homicide squad was interviewing me and Phil when they came racing into the living room.

The sight of the police cars in the driveway already had Mom and Dad in a pretty bad state. The sight of Mrs. Patterson under the den didn't help them feel better.

We spent the night at the Holiday Inn, compliments of the police. It took them a full day to finish at the house. We got a spiffy new carpet, too. The old one was carted away as evidence.

Mom and Dad heard the whole story and Mrs. Patterson finally got a decent burial. Dad had no problem going back to the house, but it took Mom a while to feel comfortable again. She kept asking me if I felt anything strange. I told her I didn't.

Which wasn't the whole truth. I don't feel anything strange, but I do feel something. Sometimes, when I'm in the den, the rocking chair starts swaying, just a bit. It's as if there's someone in it, someone who is, I'm sure, smiling. At one time, Mrs. Patterson couldn't leave. Now I don't think she wants to. I think she likes it here.